About the Author

JOHN BINGHAM—aka Lord Clanmorris, aka Michael Ward—was
born in 1908 near York, England.
The only son of the Sixth Baron
Clanmorris, he began his writing
career as a journalist. Shortly
before the outbreak of World
War II, Bingham joined the Royal
Engineers, and it was during a
train ride through the countryside that he overheard a conversation in German between two
people in his car. The couple
were observing and taking notes on the location of military instal-
lations and possible munitions factories. Pretending to be German,
Bingham spoke with them, obtaining their names and whereabouts
they were staying, which he passed on to a friend in Intelligence.
He was soon recruited by MI5, where he worked with famed un-
dercover agent Maxwell Knight, as well as David Cornwell (also
known as author John le Carré), and remained with MI5 in various
capacities well into the 1970s.

John Bingham's first novel was *My Name Is Michael Sibley,*
published in 1952; *Five Roundabouts to Heaven* followed in 1953. In
the span of thirty years, while with MI5, Bingham wrote seventeen
crime novels and thrillers, including *The Third Skin, Night's Black
Agent, A Fragment of Fear,* and *I Love, I Kill.* Bingham died in 1988.

Also by John Bingham

My Name Is Michael Sibley

The Third Skin

The Paton Street Case

Marion

Murder Plan 6

Night's Black Agent

A Case of Libel

The Double Agent

I Love, I Kill

Vulture in the Sun

God's Defector

The Marriage Bureau Murders

Deadly Picnic

Brock

Brock and the Defector

John Bingham

A Fragment
of Fear

with an introduction by
John le Carré

SIMON & SCHUSTER PAPERBACKS
NEW YORK LONDON TORONTO SYDNEY

Simon & Schuster
1230 Avenue of the Americas
New York, NY 10020

First Simon & Schuster trade paperback edition July 2007

SIMON & SCHUSTER and colophon are registered trademarks
of Simon & Schuster, Inc.

Designed by Davina Mock-Maniscalco

Manufactured in the United States of America

10 9 8 7 6 5 4 3 2 1

Library of Congress Cataloging-in-Publication Data

Bingham, John, 1908–
A fragment of fear / John Bingham with an introduction by John Le Carré.—1st Simon
& Schuster trade paperback ed.
p. cm.
I. Title.

PR6053.L283F73 2007
823'.914—dc22

For information about special discounts for bulk purchases,
please contact Simon & Schuster Special Sales at 1-800-456-6798
or business@simonandschuster.com.

ISBN-13: 978-1-4165-4048-9
ISBN-10:   1-4165-4048-2

Introduction

BY JOHN LE CARRÉ

This novel comprises some of the best work of an extremely gifted and perhaps under-regarded British crime novelist, now dead, whom I would dearly like to have called my friend. And for a time, John and I were indeed close friends. We came from totally different worlds, worked together in perfect harmony in an operational section of MI5 for two years but parted a few years later, on John's side, on terms of bitter animosity. If John had been able to hate anyone for long, he would have hated me. That we had been friends and colleagues only added spleen. John had been my professional mentor. He had been one of two men who had gone into the making of my character George Smiley. Nobody who knew John and the work he was doing could have missed the description of Smiley in my first novel, *Call for the Dead*. "Short, fat and of a quiet disposition, he appeared to spend a lot of money on really bad clothes . . ."

John had introduced me to his agent, Peter Watt, and his British publisher, Victor Gollancz. John had encouraged me to write, and read the manuscript of my first novel. John, in other words, by every generous means available to him, had set me on course to become a writer. And I would have been happy to credit him with all this—if our service had allowed me to—and probably I would have dedicated a book to him and acknowledged my debt.

But John saw things quite differently. As far as he was concerned, I had repaid him by betraying everything outside his family that he held most dear in the world: his country, his Service, his colleagues, the bond he shared with his agents in the field, and by extension his own humanity. The fond apprentice had turned wrecker. In an angry foreword to his novel *The Double Agent* written three years after the publication of *The Spy Who Came in from the Cold,* John wrote as follows: "There are two schools of thought about out Intelligence Services. One school is convinced they are staffed by murderous, powerful, double-crossing cynics, the other that the taxpayer is supporting a collection of bumbling, broken-down layabouts. It is possible to think that both extremes of thought are the result of a mixture of unclear reasoning, ignorance and possibly political or temperamental wishful thinking."

No insider doubted that John was writing about me. Or that he was expressing an opinion widely shared by his contemporaries in the Service. He might of course have added that there was a third school of thought about our Intelligence Services, and that it was his own, and my crime was that I subscribed not merely to the two he mentions, but to the third also—his. John, if pressed, might also have conceded that, just as there was an anti-authoritarian rebel in *his* nature, so was there a patriotic civil servant in mine. And that the problem with secret services was the same problem that people have: they can be an awful lot of things at once, good and bad, competent, incompetent, one day indispensable, the next a hole in the head. I might also have pointed out to him that my experience of Cold War intelligence work had extended into fields of which he was fortunate to know nothing, since John had long been stuck in the groove of domestic countersubversion, whereas I had been fortunate enough to obtain a glimpse of our foreign operations. John was sweetly unaware of the disastrous influence of James Jesus Angleton's spy mania upon the international intelligence community. He knew nothing of black operations at home or overseas. He knew nothing of the training and infiltration and deaths of uncounted armies of small spies against the communist menace. He knew precious little of conspiracy and even less of cock-up. He ran a perfected system all his own. He cherished his agents without the smallest thought of ever betraying them or exposing them to dangers they couldn't handle. But even if John *had* conceded all this, he would never have wanted to read, let alone write, about it.

As far as he was concerned, I was a literary defector who had dragged the good name of the Service through the mud. I had supped at King Arthur's table, then sawn its legs off. In those days I had to listen to a lot of that stuff, and read it in planted reviews. But when it came from John it never failed to hurt. No good my protesting I was engaged in a literary conceit. Or that anyone who knew the secret world as we did would be the first to recognize that I had invented a completely different one. Or that I had used the secret world as a theater to describe the overt world it affected to protect. As far as John was concerned—and many others too—claims of good intent were guff. I was a shit, consigned to the ranks of other shits like Compton McKenzie, Malcolm Muggeridge and J. C. Masterman, all of whom had betrayed the Service by writing about it. Thank God Bingham never lived to see David Shayler on television. On the other hand, I wish dearly that we could have had a conversation about him.

The irreconcilable differences between Bingham and myself may tell you a bit about the conflict of generations within the Service, and a bit about John. But I would not want you for a second to imagine that he was some kind of chauvinistic fuddy-duddy. Indeed, the older I get, the more often I wonder whether he was right and I was wrong. I mean by this that, ever since some PR whiz-kid sold the secret services the notion that they should present an image of openness, they have lost more and more credibility with the public. A secret service that sets out to be loved is off its head.

And if my novels in the 60s and 70s in some way invited the opening of that door, then I wish somebody could have slammed it shut.

John was a quarter of a century older than I was. He was born into the Anglo-Irish aristocracy and married a Catholic woman of birth, a playwright. He had wandered around pre-war Europe, I expect—though no one says so—for British Intelligence. Certainly I made that assumption when I gave Smiley fragments of John's pre-war past. He spoke French and German though I never heard him do it, so I don't know how well. I know little of his childhood, but imagined that, quite unlike myself, he was born into a world of certainties that time eroded. When I came to write Smiley, I tried to give him the same faint air of loss that John carried around with him. Smiley, like John, I felt, was fighting to preserve a country that survived only in his head, and was clinging to standards long abandoned by the world around him. There was something quixotic as well as shrewd about John. Like Smiley, he was the perfect parish priest of the Old Faith. He was a superb listener. He was profoundly orthodox, but with a nice dash of heresy. He exuded stability and common sense and inspired his agents with his own gentle, old-fashioned zeal. His humanity was never put on. The best of his agents were women. He managed to see some of them almost every day of their operational lives. I could not for one second, then or now, have imagined John caught up in some devious game of bluff and counter-bluff that involved the cynical sacrifice of one of his precious agents. They were his adopted children, his little wives, his creations, his wards, his orphans. John had shared their lives with them, assuring them every day that what they were doing was absolutely vital to the nation's health. He had drunk them into near oblivion when the strains of their double life became intolerable to them. And he was back next morning with the coffee for their hangovers. In this, he was the pupil and stablemate of Maxwell Knight, another Pied Piper extraordinary of men and women looking for an unorthodox way to serve their country.

"Your wife will be spat on in the fish-queue," John told them. "Your kids will be persecuted at school. You'll be hated or at best distrusted by your neighbors as a fire-breathing Red. But the Service will be with you. We'll be walking at your side even when you can't see us. We'll be worrying about you day and night." And they believed him—for as long as upstarts like le Carré didn't tell them otherwise.

But le Carré had seen more of the new verities than John had, and far fewer of the old ones. He had not fought John's war, he had never enjoyed the conviction that he was opposing pure evil, a rare privilege conferred by the 1939–45 war, but much harder to sustain in the war between capitalism and socialism, both gone off the rails. Le Carré had emerged not from the aristocracy but from a rootless childhood of chaos and larceny. And le Carré turned Bingham the preacher of certainties into Smiley the disciple of doubt. And I don't think John, if he ever fully decoded the references, would have thanked me one bit for that compliment.

So what on earth has all this to do with the book you are about to read? you ask. It is because in my sadness, and love of John, I wish you to do him justice, not just as a British patriot and supremely able intelligence officer, but as an intuitive scholar of human motive, which is what informed the writer in him. John was not only an intelligence technician but a former journalist. He understood and loved police work. As a dedicated custodian of society he cared passionately about the containment of evil. He wasn't interested in *who*dunnit. But as a master interrogator and explorer of human motive, he wanted to know *why*dunnit and whether justice was going to be served. John's country's enemies were John's enemies, whether they were Germans trying to spy on us, communists trying to undermine the fabric of bourgeois society, or our own criminals upsetting the decent order of Britain as he dreamed and loved it. An interrogator is nothing if he is not a master of many fictions, and John was all of that. Seated before his suspect, listening to the fluctuations of the suspect's voice as well as his words, watching the body language and the tiny facial inflections, the good interrogator is subconsciously trying on stories like clothes: would *this* one fit him, or would that one fit him better? Is he this person or that person—or another person altogether? And if I were in his shoes, what would I be saying? All the time he is plumbing the possibilities of the character before him.

Bingham wrote with the authority of an extraordinarily wide experience of human beings in bizarre situations. As a novelist he was held back in part by the sheer scale of the material he disposed of and could never use, in part by the constraints quite properly imposed on him by his service; but above all by his own innate sense of "good form": a notion that died a little before he did. What drove him was a love of the citadel he was protecting and a visceral disdain for its enemies. What gave him his magic was something we look for in every writer, too often in vain: an absolute command of the internal landscape of his characters, acutely observed by a humane but wonderfully corrosive eye.

And John had one other quality that every agent runner needs: great entertainment value. Now read on.

A Fragment
of Fear

We live in a dangerous age, and this is not only because of the hydrogen bomb and high taxation.

Man has always been stalked by terror, such as medieval plagues, Mongol invasions, racial persecutions, or individual rapacity; and one might add, in passing, that to blame modern juvenile crime waves upon the uncertainty of the times is the finest piece of buck passing since Judas Iscariot's insignificant act of recognition drew limelight from the power politics of his era.

As in the past, so today, the ordinary citizen must keep his eyes skinned if he is not to go under, a victim either of the dangers he recognises daily, or of other dangers which come upon him suddenly, of which he can have little inkling until, bewildered and off guard, he is called upon to defend himself as best he can.

And a very poor best it can be on occasions.

The world is still a jungle, though the settlements are larger and the linking paths, though they vary, are mostly well made and seem deceptively safe.

By day and even by night, the peasant can normally go about his lawful avocations in safety. Yet now and again, as he struggles along the more difficult trails, he may catch a momentary glimpse of eyes in the undergrowth on either side, and hear soft movements and the snapping of twigs.

If he is an optimist, he will shrug his shoulders and take little notice, as I reacted at first.

But now I say this: the dangers change in some measure but the predators are still there, a little more subtle than in former times, though fundamentally not much—fundamentally, not much—and liable suddenly to be just as red in tooth and claw.

There is no need to take notice of these words.

Better, in some ways, to be an optimist. Better to hope for the best, as the ill-equipped peasant has been compelled to do through the ages, if life was not to become intolerable. And if, now and again, the peasant is clawed to the ground, what of it?

There are plenty more of us.

The first part of this story is simple, as such affairs go. I am a writer of crime stories, which means that the characters in my stories are mostly fictional, but occasionally the victim bears a resemblance to somebody I detest, and why not indeed? Every job has its perks. Notionally to kill one's current pet aversion is some recompense for the rest of the toil involved.

But I did not really know Lucy Dawson, and I certainly did not detest her.

Yet there she was, a victim served up, as it were, upon a plate, for although I did not know her to speak to, I had seen her several times.

She was a tall, thin woman in her seventies, with a high bridged nose, a gentle smile, and a soft cultured voice. I imagine that in England she mostly wore black, but in deference to the heat of September, south of Naples, she wore grey or pale blue dresses.

I think of her mostly in grey, sitting at a table by herself, dining by herself under the trees in the outdoor restaurant, where the hotel staff served meals during the hot season. Here an occasional lizard will run among the tables, and across the Bay the lights of Naples twinkle in the darkness.

I remember vaguely the glitter of diamond rings on her fingers, and, with more precision, a magnificent amethyst and diamond pendant which she wore on a gold chain about her neck. She wore it by day as well as in the evening, and I recall thinking that it was a bit much for daytime, and that she was doubtless reluctant to leave it in her room.

She rarely spoke to anybody, apart from exchanging the normal civilities in a courteous manner, though I know that at least two married couples, for reasons of social charity, had made conversational approaches.

She spent the four days during which we were both at the hotel either reading newspapers, which she had organised from England, or books, or going for walks along the sea road aided by a brown walking stick with a gold and ivory handle, though I heard later that she sometimes made longer excursions in a hired car.

I then left my hotel near Sorrento for a week, to visit Paestum, Cuma, and other Roman remains. I had some far-fetched idea of setting a murder at Cuma, in the dark underground cavern where Sybyl is supposed to have consulted her prophetic books, or in the sanctum of one of the Greek temples at Paestum, or in the Villa of Mysteries at Pompeii, or some such nonsense.

In my absence, the murder had been committed almost on my doorstep, or at any rate a comparatively few miles away in Pompeii.

I remember thinking that had I not known Pompeii so well from former visits, I might have been wandering around those magnificent ruins on the day she died.

When I returned to my Sorrento hotel, most of the excitement had died down. The police had been and gone. Her room, which for a period had been both sealed and locked, was now only locked, pending disposal of her belongings. The hotel guests and staff had ceased to mull over the tragedy in low voices. People swam and lay in the sun, and watched newcomers with pale skin rubbing themselves with anti-sunburn lotion. The beach umbrellas looked as gay as ever. The boat called each morning for day-trippers to Capri, and Vesuvius brooded mistily in the distance, seemingly content with the havoc he had wrought in A.D. 79.

Already, gentle, lonely Mrs. Dawson, photographed, docketed, and cleaned, was buried in the Protestant cemetery at Naples, and in the hotel it was almost as if this elegant old lady had never been there.

I had naturally read about the crime in the Italian newspapers and was puzzled as the Italian police were.

Her diamond rings and valuable amethyst pendant had not been stolen. About seven pounds' worth of Italian lire were untouched in her handbag. A sex assault was clearly out of the question.

She had been strangled with an Italian silk scarf behind the walls of House No. 27 in Section 12. She had several rather fine Italian scarves in delicate pastel shades of mingled browns and blues and yellows. I do not know which one was used to kill her.

There are a great many houses in Pompeii which are mere shells, roofless, the ruined walls of varying heights enclosing squares and rectangles of bare earth. I imagined the killer luring this old and frail woman into House No. 27, then leaning forward, perhaps with some pretext of adjusting her scarf, crossing his hands, while each held one side of the scarf, then quickly extending his hands so that the knuckles pressed suddenly into the carotid artery on each side of her neck. The suddenness and shock prevented an outcry. It is a soundless and happily painless method of causing unconsciousness in two or three seconds. Lengthier pressure causes death by continuing to cut off the supply of blood to the brain. Thus I imagined it happening.

If this method had been used, it indicated that Mrs. Dawson knew her murderer, for I could not imagine that dignified Victorian figure allowing a strange man to adjust her scarf, and for reasons of physical strength it would almost certainly have been a man.

But maybe it was a stranger, and maybe a clumsier method had been used. I hoped not.

I drove over to dusty Pompeii, not for ghoulish reasons, but because I write articles as well as books, and if at any time I wished to include this crime, it would be useful to have visited the spot and seen it with one's own eyes, and taken notes.

The visits of morbid sightseers had ceased, and I entered House No. 27 alone, though twenty yards up the street I saw a swarthy, stocky figure heave himself off a low wall and move in my direction. He was dressed in the simple uniform of the guards whose duty it is to prevent sightseers making off with such remaining Roman treasures as have not been housed in the local museum or removed to the Naples museum.

He was a rugged man of about fifty, a member of the Italian Communist Party, with whom I had had long conversations on previous occasions. Outwardly sour and embittered, inwardly, I suspect as soft as butter, he ascribed any and every misfortune he had ever suffered or would suffer to the iniquities of the capitalist system.

His name was Mario Bartelli. Mario Bartelli always conceded that Vesuvius had done a good job in that it had destroyed the capitalists in Pompeii, Herculaneum, and other towns. But the whole thing had been too parochial. What was needed was another kind of eruption, which would destroy the whole rotten decadent system. For four days before the eruption, there had been earthquake rumblings, reminiscent of an earlier disaster, giving warning to the rich spivs, the clever dicks, the idle aristocracy who had time to think and organise, and what had happened? Why were no skeletons of horses found? Because all the horses had been commandeered by the rich.

On another occasion, entertaining in his way, as is every fanatic, he blamed his paucity of tips on victimisation by the Pompeii administration.

Guards in some sections with one or two special exhibits were sure of tips. The guard in the House of the Vetii, for example, was certain to win a daily quota for unlocking the cupboard which shielded his indecorous painting from eyes which might be shocked by it.

Mario had some Roman bread ovens and corn-grinding ex-

hibits in his Section. You could see them from the pavement. No
need to hand over lire to see bread ovens and corn-grinders.

It was the same when he had the Section which included the
Amphitheatre. There were plenty of wine taverns in the Section,
and plenty of graffiti on the walls. The Romans liked a drink on the
way to and from the arena, and the drink emboldened them to
scrawl slogans on the walls. But you could see the taverns and the
graffiti for the price of the entrance ticket.

So there were no tips there either.

Guards were changed around, and so was he, but always to a
tip-less section. It was clear to Mario Bartelli that he was the victim
of anti-Communist discrimination.

For Mario, Pompeii represented meals of farinacious food and
three rooms for himself and his family in a stuffy concrete building
in Castellammare. And that was all Pompeii would ever mean to
him.

I am in love with Pompeii, but Mario Bartelli hates the whole
hot, arid dump. For him the problems of the present obliterate the
past more effectively than Vesuvius has ever done.

As he approached and I went into the house where Mrs. Dawson had been killed, I could not help reflecting upon the unroman-
tic conditions in which most murdered people are found: the
deserted outhouse on a chicken farm, the crumpled sheets of the
sickroom with the chipped crockery which contained the poison;
the bramble bushes by the side of the muddy lane.

At Pompeii the surroundings were unique enough, but the uninteresting bare patch of parched earth and the sky into which the
sightless eyes had gazed made it desolately similar to the scene of
many another intolerable end.

I turned as Mario came in through the entrance of House No.
27 and for a moment I thought his soured and lined face showed
some fleeting expression of pleasure, but I may have been mistaken. He crossed himself, Communist or not, in response to some
deep-seated subconscious prompting, and I could tell from the
glance of his eyes in which corner Mrs. Dawson's body had been
found.

For it was Mario Bartelli who had found her, twenty-four hours after her death, and for once he was on guard in a Section in which tips, from journalists and tourists, flowed freely.

We had a long talk together, and from what he said, and from what I knew of his character, I was able to form what I believe to be an accurate picture of the events of that terrible morning of September 11th. This I will put on record, for even now after some considerable time, I am not certain what the future holds for me.

At ten o'clock on the morning of September 11th the sun was already very hot. Mario Bartelli was seated on a low ruined wall almost opposite No. 27, in the shade cast by an adjacent house. He extinguished a cheap State-manufactured cigarette and put the butt in a tin box for subsequent re-rolling with other cigarette ends.

He idly watched Aldo, the guide, go past with a small party of American tourists, and, I have no doubt, wished them all ill, including Aldo, who consistently refused to join the Communist Party of Italy.

A moment or two later, he saw Aldo and his party cross the street a few yards away, going over from one steeply built pavement to another, walking clumsily on the great stepping-stones which at intervals link the two sides. Aldo paused, as he always did at this spot, pointing out the deep ruts in the roadway caused by the wheels of Roman chariots. Aldo's voice droned on:

"It is often said, ladies and gentlemen, that Pompeii was destroyed by the eruption of Vesuvius on August the twenty-fourth, in the year A.D. seventy-nine. You have now seen that this is not true. Thanks to the lava and volcanic dust, Pompeii and Herculaneum were, in fact, *preserved* by the eruption, so that here, as nowhere else in the world, we can see how those old-time Romans lived their lives."

I imagine that at this point Mario Bartelli spat, thinking that he, too, could be a guide and earn fat tips except that they wouldn't much like what he would say.

"Two thousand people, to our certain knowledge, and probably more in the surrounding countryside, died during that terrible eruption," droned Aldo. "Many were slaves looting the property of their owners."

Doubtless, Mario Bartelli stirred irritably thinking bitterly that the slaves were in fact only retrieving the wealth which had been filched from their class. It was military action at its best. He heard Aldo's voice rise as he reached his peroration.

"In a letter to Tacitus, ladies and gentlemen, Pliny the Younger, who was in nearby Misenum, said the world became quite black, not merely like a dark night, but like a room without windows. At one moment the sky was clear. Suddenly there was a loud and terrible crack, and gradually the sky darkened with stones and ashes. The sea receded, stranding maritime creatures. At first there was a horrible black cloud, rent by shafts of darting flames. Fleeing chariots, on seemingly flat ground, were rocked and flung about like toys, so that even heavy stones could not keep them steady. People screamed and called to each other in the gathering gloom. Apart from the looting slaves, there were others who stayed in Pompeii. The sick and infirm. Those who hoped it would quickly pass and remained in their homes.

"Those homes, ladies and gentlemen, were buried to a depth of many metres, and those people who were not crushed by falling walls and pillars were killed by the foul poisonous fumes which accompanied the ashes. And in the end there was no escape. Only death in the darkness which was like a room without windows."

This bit was always Aldo's great moment. I have myself heard his performance, and very fine it is, his voice rising and falling with simulated fervour. When he came to the last sentence he always spoke in a low tragic voice, hardly louder than a whisper, and followed it with a silence, as if in memory of those who had died.

It was at this point, and while he was weighing in his mind the words of Lenin, who said that in certain circumstances one could have a peaceful transition to Socialism, that Mario Bartelli saw the white butterfly, lost in the nectarless wastes of Pompeii, and a girl of about nine who had lagged behind Aldo's party, and was trying to catch the insect.

Like most Italians, Mario loved children.

He watched as the butterfly settled on a stone and the child cautiously approached, and he smiled when the butterfly escaped at the last moment.

He was delighted. Jumbled thoughts went through his mind. There had been the cruelties of a slave-owning community, the terror of the arena, the sulphurous darkness of the eruption, the centuries of silence and death; and now there was sunshine again, and the dainty white butterfly playing with this healthy, pink-faced little girl.

It restored your faith in the triumph of good over evil, he thought awkwardly, or told me he did.

He slowly walked towards the entrance to House No. 27, into which the child and butterfly had gone, hoping to see more of the chase, and staggered as the child hurtled out again and into his knees.

He bent to pick her up, saying, "What is it?" but she eluded him, and ran down the street, and fell once, as she crossed the stepping-stones to the other side where her parents were still listening to Aldo; and she picked herself up, and ran on, without bothering to brush the dust from her grazed knees, until she had flung herself into her mother's arms.

He saw Aldo and the tourists gather round the girl, and he himself became suddenly aware of a loud thrumming noise, and turning he saw a dense cloud of flies above the wall which divided the front and the back rooms of House No. 27. So he went behind the dividing wall, and then came back again to the street, and leaned over the low outer wall, and croaked for air. As the sickness passed he heard running footsteps, and Aldo the guide joined him.

Mario Bartelli said: "Don't go in! It is a matter for the police."

But Aldo shook him off and went in. When he came back Mario Bartelli said:

"Stand at the entrance here and don't let anybody in. I will run down to the Administration and report."

Aldo said: "I will go if you wish. Smoke a cigarette. I will go."

Mario shook his head. It was his duty to report personally all unusual incidents and irregularities in his Section.

He turned and hastened along the street, still feeling sick, half walking, half running, past the Forum, and down the street that sloped to the tunnel called the Porta Marina, and out of the twilight of the tunnel into the sunshine again, past the vendors of postcards and souvenirs, and so, perspiring, to the Administration building near the railway station.

During part of the way he thought about the child.

It was not good for a small girl to see a thing like that. It could give her nightmares.

Only a thin, ruined wall had divided innocence and fun from evil and death.

The dainty butterfly had led her in, and then flown heartlessly on. He hoped she would not have nightmares. He was afraid she would but he hoped she wouldn't. He told me that these were his thoughts, and they probably were.

He was a kindly man at heart, though he did his best to hide the fact.

After hearing of these things from Bartelli, I returned to my hotel, and after dinner when darkness had fallen, I watched the little boats creep round the coast of the Bay of Naples, as Lucy Dawson had done, the crews fishing with lantern and hand harpoon. From the inland villages, the fireworks of the harvest festivals echoed round the mountains like gunfire. I imagined how in Pompeii the night guards were languidly patrolling, meeting, chatting, and passing on. It is easier to break into a bank, these days, than to steal the remaining Roman treasures of Pompeii.

The moon doubtless shone on the Forum and on the rising tiers of seats in the Amphitheatre, and on the House of the Mysteries, and on the Street of Tombs, turning the colour of the bricks to a pale cream, and upon the piece of bare ground on which Lucy Dawson had lain, unrobbed, her jewellery glittering, while alarm at her failure to return spread through the other hotel guests.

I got up and strolled into the hotel and made my way to the bar and ordered a cognac. Bruno, the barman, was talking to the proprietor, Signor Bardoni, a short, thick-set man with a jutting chin, known secretly to the staff as the Duce, and less reverently to the visitors as Musso.

Bardoni greeted me politely, and so he should have done, considering the prices he charged.

"And did you have a good trip, Signor Compton?" he said in English.

I shrugged, and replied in Italian. I did not like Bardoni.

"So-so. I have a notebook full of notes. It was hot. I felt like a cross between an architect and an estate agent taking an inventory."

"It seems that you did not need to move very far for a murder story. You have heard, of course?"

I nodded and took a sip of brandy.

"When was she buried?"

"Two days ago. In the Protestant cemetery at Naples. A sad business. Not good for the tourist trade."

"I doubt if millions of British people will cease to visit Italy because one old lady was murdered."

"People are funny, Signor."

"Not as funny as that."

"We must hope not," he said, indifferently. The subject was petering out, and that suited me. But as an afterthought I said:

"Were there any Italian people at the funeral?"

"Only me, Signor, representing the hotel. She had often visited us. I took a wreath on behalf of the staff—and of the other guests, of course."

He had small, dark eyes, and the formation of the face around them was curiously hard, so that one had the impression that the sockets had been chopped out of wood.

I noted the chin jutting out more than usual, and the way his eyes looked straight into mine. People have grown accustomed to the cliché about shifty characters who cannot look you straight in the face, and so have the shifty characters; so much so that I have found that when a person now looks you straight in the eyes, as he speaks, it is often a damned good reason to think he is telling you a whopper.

I thought that Bardoni was probably lying now, and that he had not bothered to go.

"Any of the guests from the hotel go?"

"Signor, I did not tell them about it. Why should I? They come here for holidays, not funerals."

"Anybody from England fly out to Naples?"

He was in a bit of a spot now, of course, because, if he hadn't attended himself, he wouldn't know.

"The fare is expensive, and last minute tickets hard to get," he murmured tactfully with a sigh. He looked at his watch, muttered something about a telephone call, and left me. It was a neat evasion of the question. I guessed that as far as Bardoni was concerned Lucy Dawson had ceased to be a paying proposition, and was therefore of no account, from the moment when the scarf was tightened round her throat.

"I do not think Mrs. Dawson had any family left," I heard Bruno say.

He was a different type from Bardoni. He was a tall, soft-spoken young man, with copper-coloured hair and grey eyes, and a friendly desire to please everybody.

I nodded and finished my brandy.

"Poor old soul," I said.

"Poor old lady," agreed Bruno.

I was right about Bardoni not going to the funeral. But I was wrong about the reason. In a negative sort of way, Mrs. Dawson was a paying proposition for Bardoni from the moment she died.

~~~

The following morning I still had a fixation about old Mrs. Lucy Dawson being buried by bored Italian gravediggers, after a scraped-up service by the local chaplain, the funds advanced against her estate by the British Consulate, and not a soul to wish her farewell, and not a flower thrown on the grave. And all that sort of stuff. I can be sentimental to the point of sentimentality, given half a chance. Not that it usually lasts very long.

I swam in the clear sea during part of the morning, watched a little shoal of grey fish butting their noses inquisitively against my legs when I stood upright; and I lay in the sun and read; and had a couple of iced Cinzanos before lunch.

In the afternoon I had to go into Naples to verify some facts at the National Museum, and while I was in the little electric coastal train which swayed its way past Pompeii along to Napoli–Vesuvio Station I had another nasty attack of sentimentality, and knew what I would do when I had completed my business at the museum.

So in the late afternoon I bought a bunch of red and white carnations, hired a taxi, and drove to the cemetery. The cemetery keeper, with suitable words of dismay at the cause of her death, showed me her grave. I laid the carnations on the grave without a card, because in the circumstances I couldn't think of anything suitable to write.

There was one other wreath on the bare soil, a rather sumptuous affair made up mostly of gladioli, the flowers now sad and faded in the sun. I bent over to read the inscription on the card, sorry that I had done Bardoni an injustice, and found I hadn't.

The card simply said: *From the Stepping Stones in memory of happier times.* Some small type in the bottom left-hand corner read: Trans-Continental Flowers Ltd.

I had heard of some shaggy-looking singers called the Rolling Stones, but the Stepping Stones meant nothing to me.

Still, it meant that somebody, probably in England, had had the thought to wire some flowers for the funeral. It also meant that somebody, probably in England, knew when the burial was to take place, though the significance of this was not and could not be apparent to me at the time.

What with the carnations, the taxi, and a tip to the cemetery-keeper, the expedition had cost me rather over two pounds.

I sometimes think it was the worst spent money I have ever laid out.

CHAPTER 2

Juliet and I were due to be married on October 16th, and it might seem odd that we were separated. The reasons are simple enough. I was in Italy because I had had a bit of a battering in a car accident. There was no permanent damage, but a couple of weeks in hospital while the bits and pieces mended had left me pale and under the weather. I was not sleeping very well for one thing. So the doctor had recommended sun, swimming, and all the rest of those things which trip so easily off the medical tongue.

Juliet, on the other hand, had to go to America as a secretary attached to a government delegation and attend conferences. So we separated for a month, with moans and sighs, and all the appropriate agony.

As a result of conference delays she was not now able to return before October 11th, which would mean a hectic few days before the wedding. I stayed in Italy till October 2nd.

During the last few days I developed my "thing" about old Mrs. Dawson. I was writing up the odd descriptive paragraph based on my notes, and kidding myself that I was doing some work. But of course I wasn't. Not really. I was swimming and sunbathing, and strolling along the little roads, peering in at cottages among the vines and lemon trees, and reading, and breakfasting late in my pyjamas on the balcony overlooking the sea. I hadn't a care in the world, but plenty of time to think.

Everybody knows that when everything is going well, and there is not a cloud in the sky, then that is the time to watch out, because such conditions are not normal in this troubled life, and can't last. One pays lip service to such platitudes, but that is about all. As far as Juliet and I were concerned, we were both healthy, in love, and solvent, and I had no morbid premonitions.

I had no firm plot for my next book, but I knew that would come. I was not worried. My mind was, in a way, a sort of vacuum, and into the vacuum seeped this "thing" about Lucy Dawson.

What kept worrying me, as I am sure it did the Italian police, was the fact that she had not been robbed. Every explanation I invented could easily be faulted.

The man had planned to rob her, but suddenly thought he was about to be disturbed and had left hurriedly. (But he could have returned.) Or he had had an inhibition about robbing a dead body, thinking it might bring ill luck. (Then why kill her? Murder is not for sensitive souls.) So it went on.

Meanwhile her room remained locked on the instructions of the Italian police, and pending action by the British Consulate to remove her belongings; which I expect annoyed Bardoni because he couldn't let it.

Two days before I left the hotel to fly back to London I had what I then thought, in my ignorance, was a stroke of luck. I wandered back from a mid-morning swim in my towelling wrap. It was somewhere about eleven o'clock, and I thought I would change and do an hour or so's work before the pre-lunch drink.

I trudged up from the sandy beach and through the hotel vestibule, my leather bathing shoes slapping on the gleaming tiled floor, then up the uncarpeted wooden staircase to the first floor, and along the corridor to my room.

On the way, I had to pass Mrs. Dawson's room. I remember I was thinking about the malarial conditions which had finally caused the Greek settlements to abandon the temples at Paestum when I noted that her door was ajar.

I paused and listened.

There was no movement inside the room. I heard faint voices from below in the hotel, and from outside the cries of swimmers and people playing tennis, but they seemed filtered, like echoes from far away.

I gently pushed the door open.

In the sunlight which percolated through the half-opened jalousies I saw a bucket and a mop near the doorway, and guessed that the hotel management had decided, police or no police, Consulate or no Consulate, that the room should be cleaned. Sophia would be doing the cleaning. She cleaned my room, and all the others along the corridor, a plump, cheerful little dark-skinned woman of about thirty-five. Either she had left earlier than usual to have her mid-day meal, or she had forgotten some cleaning material, or had gone to fetch some more.

I guessed I could handle Sophia, yet when I went in I trod as softly as my beach shoes would allow—perhaps because I had a slightly guilty conscience, knowing I should not be there; perhaps because of the associations of the room with the dead woman; perhaps a bit of both.

Two vases of flowers were on the built-in dressing-table. The roses were dead, but the gladioli still had some red at their tips which had not yet quite faded.

Two monogrammed Edwardian silver hairbrushes were set neatly beside the vases and two silver boxes with intricately worked edges, a glass powder bowl with a silver top and two ebony clothes brushes with silver initials. On the washbasin shelf were one or two medicine bottles, a bottle of aspirins and a small pill box.

At the back of the door her beige-coloured tweed travelling coat was hanging. Over it hung one of her pastel-coloured chiffon scarves.

Still laid out on the bed was her silk night-dress—old-fashioned, with inset lace and hand embroidery. Yet although it looked well worn the silk was still thick and strong.

Outside, in the tiny anteroom, the wardrobe was full of her clothes; unexceptionable print dresses, blouses, and cotton skirts. Four or five pairs of sandals and neat walking shoes were placed in a row on the floor of the cupboard.

I went into the tiled bathroom and noted her mauve silk dressing-gown, her toothbrush in its place, and a large tablet of bathsoap in the soap dish. I picked it up. Like her clothes the soap was unexceptionable. I think it was jasmine.

I walked back into the bedroom and opened the dressing-table drawer. Face cream, lip-salve, a nail-case in mauve leather, some corn plasters, a pair of curling tongs, hairgrips and hairpins. Handkerchiefs in an embroidered sachet. On the night table there were three books—a biography of Edward VII, two Tauchnitz editions of modern novels, two maps and a guide to Naples.

As I looked round the room, a slight wind moved the thick, blue woven curtains. The dust on the tiled floor and the faded flowers on the dressing-table spoke of neglect and loss, but the voices from the beach still filtered from another life, and through the windows I could see the waiters moving about behind the cactus hedge, under the pine trees, setting the tables for lunch. Their white coats made patches of light against the bright reds, the yellows, the greens and blues of the fringed tablecloths.

I was eager now to be out of the room with its half-light and depression, even a little impatient with myself for entering, and I made for the door.

As I did so, I passed a small table by the windows. On it lay a camera, a tin of English biscuits, her passport, a cheque-book, one of those imitation leather covers which hold travellers' cheques and a most sumptuously produced book on Pompeii and Herculaneum.

I could not resist picking up the book. It was beautifully illustrated, the photographs taken by a camera artist. At the back of the book, before the pages of the index and bibliography, was a slim Italian bookmark in tooled leather. It had been inserted at the map page showing the lay-out of each street and house in Pompeii. Almost automatically I looked for House No. 27 in Section 2. I found it fairly easily, for the simple reason that somebody, presumably Mrs. Dawson, had marked the site with a small cross in pencil. She had done more. She had traced the route, lightly in pencil, from the Porta Marina, past the Forum, to Section 12 and right up to the house.

She knew where she was going all right.

She had carefully marked the way to her own death. Almost certainly, then, she knew whom she was to meet, which would have made things easier for whoever adjusted her scarf; if you could call it adjusting her scarf.

I am amazed now at the importance I attached to these piffling details at the time and how clever I thought I was.

The evening before I left for London I went to the reception desk and asked for my bill. Alfredo, an olive-skinned Sicilian, was on duty, a pleasant, affable young man of good family, I should say, who was gaining experience in the hotel business by working in various departments. All Italian hotel bills, presented in lire, look like calculated distances in light-years to some distant star. I joked with him about State tax and local tax and service charge, and added a facetious remark, in rather poor taste, which I instantly regretted:

"I hope for Signor Bardoni's sake that poor Mrs. Dawson had paid her bill."

"I could not say," said Alfredo. "Mrs. Dawson always paid her money direct to Signor Bardoni. It was an eccentricity. Perhaps she did not quite trust our mathematics," he added a little tartly.

"Elderly English ladies sometimes develop these odd habits," I said soothingly.

I glanced down at the bill with its astronomic-looking total. The details meant nothing to me, and never do, especially those on the little chits attached to the bill, written in indecipherable hieroglyphics, and dealing with items such as wines, bar drinks, soda water, laundry, car hire, room service, etc., most of them long past and uncheckable.

I looked through the chits in a dazed kind of way, but I was not thinking about them. I was finally facing the fact that I wanted to build up Mrs. Dawson as a person. I wanted to know more about her.

She had become my pet victim. The one who was killed but not robbed, either of her jewellery, her money, or her virtue.

"Can you give me her address in England?" I said, suddenly.

Alfredo's mind was on other things.

"Whose address, sir?"

"Mrs. Dawson's."

Signor Bardoni had a light tread. I did not know he was behind me. He said:

"I can give you her address, Mr. Compton, if you come into my office."

I followed him into his little office, with its tiled floor, modern desk and chairs and filing cabinets.

"Sit down, Mr. Compton."

I sat down and offered him a cigarette, but he refused it. He did not need to refer to any papers. He knew her address. He said: "In England she lived at the Bower Hotel, Burlington-on-Sea, Sussex. If you had asked me that I would have told you. It was not necessary to go into her room to try to find out, Mr. Compton."

His chair behind the big desk was higher than mine, which can be annoying if one knows one is in the wrong. He lit a cigar, pulling at it vigorously. Through the blue smoke I saw his eyes watching my face from their wooden sockets.

For the first time in this affair I caught a whiff of hostility. It was something more than that of a hotel proprietor gently reproving a guest for a misdemeanour. I am very sensitive, not merely to atmosphere, but to shades of atmosphere.

"I was not looking for her address, Mr. Bardoni. I was—"

He cut me short.

"It could have been very embarrassing for me—and for you, if the police had heard about it."

"I happened to be passing her room, and saw the door ajar."

"Many guests leave their doors ajar, Mr. Compton. It is not usually regarded as an invitation to look round their rooms."

The rebuke was open and undisguised.

"This guest is permanently away from her room," I said coldly.

"Mr. Compton, her possessions are still in my care. I am responsible for them."

I got up out of my chair.

"I am not suggesting anything, Mr. Compton, naturally not, except perhaps to point out that to meddle in matters in which the police of this country are already engaged, either now or even in the future, can perhaps lead to trouble, and even pain for innocent people."

He was on his feet, too, now, and moving to the door to open it for me. He said:

"Real life people are real life people, and story-book people are story-book people. Better and easier to keep the two apart, is it not?"

His voice suddenly dropped, and he spoke softly and persuasively, and none can do this better than the Italians:

"Better to allow this poor English lady to rest at peace. Her life has run its course, Mr. Compton, with all its trials and tribulations. Her soul has departed, and her body sleeps in our Italian soil which she loved so dearly. Do not create from her sad ghost some distorted character for a book. Agreed?"

He was hammering it up, of course, though to some effect. I hesitated. But he couldn't leave well alone. As he opened the door he added:

"Let her be, Mr. Compton, let her be! If not for her sake then for your own, for sometimes the dead can hit back!"

It was the cheap threat in those corny words about the dead hitting back which destroyed the earlier effect of his words. As I went out, I said:

"While she was alive her affairs were her own. But now the manner of her death has made her, in some measure, the concern and even the property of us all."

As a rejoinder it was pretty corny, too, though at the moment, as an off-the-cuff retort, it seemed a nicely rounded phrase.

But like Bardoni, I could not leave well alone. The temptation was too much and I had to have another crack at him.

"I took some flowers to the grave yesterday. The wreath from the hotel staff and guests must have faded, and been removed, since it was not there."

He stood by the door, soft persuasiveness gone, his entire face now looking as though it had been carved out of wood, not just his eye sockets.

"None of our flowers left on the grave?" he said. "How sad. How unfortunate the sun has been so hot."

"There was one wreath, from England, from some people called the Stepping Stones," I murmured indifferently. "And now I will go and pay your bill."

He bowed. I bade him good night. He did not respond. I did not care. I didn't like him enough to care. In fact, I cordially disliked him for the way he had reproved me about the room. In fact, for two pins I would have had a damned good row with him.

If I had been listening acutely, I might now have heard the first faint rustle in the undergrowth, even caught the first glint of green eyes. But I wasn't. I ascribed his attempt to dissuade me from taking an interest in Lucy Dawson to some vague idea of circumventing bad publicity for his hotel. I was, if anything, more determined than ever to find out further details about the woman, and even to write an article or two as soon as possible, mentioning his hotel in a disparaging though non libellous way.

So the peasant quickened his steps, poor optimistic ignoramus, and within a few days of my return to England I went down to Burlington, Sussex.

There is nothing unusual about the Bower Hotel, Burlington-on-Sea. It stands as it has stood for eighty years, gazing mournfully at the Channel across the narrow promenade.

To the right and left of it other grey buildings were dripping in the rain when I went down there. Some of them were small and did not aspire to the title of hotel. All of them, with one or two exceptions, provided a bed and food of a sort for those who wished to live or stay at Burlington. There was a surprising number of such people. Some came voluntarily there to spend their holidays, because it had a strip of sand for children, at least when the tide was low, and a short pier, a few cinemas and two dance halls.

Others, elderly people, lived in the hotels and boarding houses for as long during the year as they were permitted to do so. Most of them curried favour with the proprietors and thought they were popular with them, and so they were to some extent, particularly in winter, since they paid the running costs of the establishment. Had it not been for the permanent residents, as they were politely called, the proprietors would have had to close each autumn, and engage fresh staff each spring, which is no small problem.

But when spring and summer arrived, the love of the proprietors for their permanent residents wore thin. Most of the residents couldn't afford to pay high summer prices for their rooms. Most of them weren't allowed to stay on, even if they could.

Elderly residents can only pay rent while they are alive. They don't live for ever. If they hang around occupying their rooms all the summer how does the place get known? What about fresh blood, and particularly holiday-makers' blood?

Thus argued Miss Constance Brett, I learned, who ruled the Bower Hotel like an eastern potentate, and wasn't much tougher, some said, than an old bayonet scabbard.

So every Easter or Whitsun there was an exodus from Burlington. It consisted of the old, the frail, the lame and the impoverished; and all over the country relatives prepared spare rooms, and proprietors of crumby places inland partially aired the damp beds in preparation for the Burlington refugees.

In the autumn the residents were allowed to come back and sometimes even occupy their old rooms. In return for the privilege of paying out good money, they could forget the worries of the summer. They had been taken back.

Familiar rooms, surroundings, and faces made it seem like home. They were grateful, and often said so, which was more than the proprietors ever did, because it is bad policy to unbend too much with subject races such as permanent residents.

The Bower Hotel, owing to the grey stones of which it was built, and its architecture, must have looked sad from the moment when the first Victorian customer crossed the threshold. It gave the impression of a hotel which never wanted to be there. In this it was deceptive, like some of the staff, and some of the residents. For unlike its seedier neighbours, which were mere converted houses, the Bower had been built as a hotel in the first place. So had the George Hotel, further along the promenade, and the Cliff Hotel, above the town, but they were giants, with American Bars and orchestras, and in a different class altogether.

Nevertheless, the Bower had class, too, of its kind. It lay back a few yards from the road and there was a short drive with an entrance for cars marked IN, and another marked OUT.

Inside the metal-studded front door, there was a reception-desk on the right, where a grey-haired, bespectacled woman, called Miss Banks, appeared to pore over ledgers from eight o'clock in the morning until six o'clock at night, with an hour off for lunch. Framed on the wall above Miss Banks' head was an embroidered sampler which those arrivals who had only known the exterior of the hotel regarded with some astonishment:

> A thing of beauty is a joy for ever;
> Its loveliness increases; it will never
> Pass into nothingness; but still will keep
> A *BOWER* quiet for us, and a sleep
> Full of sweet dreams, and health, and quiet breathing.
> —John Keats

On the left of the entrance hall was the hall porter's desk, with railway time-tables and brochures, and behind the porter's stool a series of pigeon-holes for letters and keys.

The hotel was heavily carpeted throughout, and comfortably furnished, and most of the rooms had central heating. Even the food was reasonable. So that despite its melancholy exterior it was snug inside. Miss Brett, who had been running it for nineteen years, knew her job. Most of her residents were allowed to stay during the summer if they could afford the increased seasonal prices, though not all, and she saw to it that their creature comforts were well attended to.

Above all, she kept them warm. Too warm for a casual visitor like myself. My mother lived in a very different type of hotel near Brighton, friendly and cheerful, on the outside as well as inside, with plenty of daylight flooding in through the big windows, and here, too, I have found the heat somewhat overpowering. But then elderly people have thin blood.

Food is taken seriously at these hotels, and though hardly any of the residents take any exercise, most of them eat four meals a day and have a tin of biscuits by the bedside to keep them going till dawn. During the two nights and three days I spent at the Bower I learned that the only bad mistake Miss Brett ever made in her early days was to try to economise on food. The complaints nearly cost her her job.

The Bower Hotel, with its overheated rooms and sombre exterior, was not merely a home for many. It was a kind of club where each member treated the others with politeness and dignity, where each had a secure niche of greater or lesser importance.

It was easy for me to feel patronising about this little community but I tried not to. The club was a refuge from loneliness and despair for a vanishing generation ill suited to modern conditions.

It was an enclave in which there were smooth waters, where sails were easily trimmed to any light breezes which might from time to time arise. Such thunder as was heard came only distantly, from the noisy, brash, modern hinterland, and any lightning was of the harmless, flickering summer type.

The Bower Hotel was not fitted to withstand forked lightning of the killer variety.

I arrived in time for lunch, and sought an interview with Miss Constance Brett immediately after the meal.

She was a heavily built woman of about fifty, with iron grey hair cut in an old-fashioned bobbed style, a muddy complexion, a square face, and pale blue eyes. She was dressed in a brown blouse, a dark grey cardigan, a skirt of a lighter grey, thick beige stockings, low heeled shoes, and wore a single row of large, cheap, pink, artificial pearls.

The big square ashtray on her desk by the window was half filled with cigarette stubs. I judged her a woman whom no man had loved. The hotel was her empire. Her living-room, which was half-office, and the bedroom, which I glimpsed through a partly opened door, was her home. The respect of her staff and the flattery of the residents were her substitutes for affection.

I explained to her my purpose, adding for good measure that in my view the case was unlikely to be solved, and I wished to write about it for criminological interest and record, perhaps in a book of unsolved murders, under the heading of *The Pompeiian Murder.*

"I knew Mrs. Dawson only slightly, but she told me how happy she had been at the Bower," I said, to try and soften her up. I could have saved myself the trouble.

"This is very irregular you know," Miss Brett said abruptly.

"She's dead, Miss Brett. I understand she had no family left. Who can object?"

She did not reply at once. Then she said:

"I've answered many questions already for the police. I'm depressed and tired of it all."

"I can understand that. Signor Bardoni, manager at the Sorrento hotel, felt the same. When he confirmed this address he said he was sure you would do your best," I lied.

"Did he indeed?"

She was looking at me with her pale, emotionless eyes. I noticed a slight flush at the lower part of her neck, and how it was spreading slowly up her throat.

"Do you know him?" I asked.

"No, I don't know him. I met him once, but I don't know him. A few years ago, after Mrs. Dawson had booked a room at his hotel, and had been unwell, he apparently wrote to her and said that he was coming to England and would be returning to Italy at about the same time as she was going there. He would pick her up here and look after her on the journey, which he did. I just met him briefly."

"That was kind of him."

"Yes, it was." There was no enthusiasm in her voice. "You're not a private detective, are you?"

"A private detective? Good God, no! Why should I be? Who would employ me, and why, for heaven's sake?"

"I just wondered."

"Why should I be a private detective?" I persisted.

She stubbed out her cigarette in the square ashtray, and looked out of the window across the grey Channel.

She was an ugly, ungracious woman, and difficult to talk to. I felt an appalling pity for her, encased and protected as she was by her impenetrable unattractiveness. I could not understand why she had flushed when I mentioned Bardoni, but I knew that nobody, and certainly not a worldly Italian, was likely to have had a brief whirlwind flirtation with her. She did not reply directly to my question.

"You are just an author—well, what do you want to know?"

Before I could pose a question she said:

"Mrs. Dawson was a very remarkable woman."

"I'm sure she was. How long had she been living here?"

"About seventeen years."

"Perhaps you could tell me something of her background?"

"It is not my business to inquire into the background of a resident."

I got up from my chair and walked over to the window. I looked down at the promenade, allowing time for my irritation to die. I wasn't going to get far with this one.

"What happened to her husband?" I asked perfunctorily.

"He died many years ago. There was some tragedy."

"What sort of tragedy?"

"I haven't the faintest idea. It is not for me to pry into personal tragedies."

"Had she any family left?"

"I don't think so."

"Had she any close friends in the hotel?"

She hesitated. I suppose she knew I could find out, anyway. She said:

"Well, there was Mrs. Gray, who came here at about the same time. And Mrs. Dacey, I suppose, because she has been here almost as long, though she keeps herself to herself."

"Had she any hobbies or eccentricities?"

"Not as far as I know."

"Is there anything interesting about her at all which you can tell me?"

"Nothing."

I paused.

"Then why was she a very remarkable woman, Miss Brett?"

I stared at her as I spoke, and saw the pink flush start again in her throat and spread painfully upwards.

"She just was. She was more active than most of our elderly residents."

"That's all?"

"Yes, that's all."

I thanked her. As I moved towards the door, she said:

"Why ferret about in the past, Mr. Compton?"

She had risen to her feet and stood by her desk, sturdy, ugly, and in some odd way defiant. Once again I felt a wave of pity, as one does sometimes for unlovable or unlikable people. It's not that one wants to love them or even like them. There are only twenty-four hours in the day. You can't take them all on.

"It won't do any good, will it?" she added.

I repeated my earlier reply:

"What harm will it do?"

She walked heavily toward the windows. She was not particularly masculine but she had no feminine appeal. She was a lump of humanity mechanised into the hotel business.

"Delving into the past—what good will it do?" she said helplessly, without looking round.

"What harm?" I said yet again. "I don't understand—what's the harm?"

The change from hostility to something akin to a plea had caught me by surprise.

"None, I suppose," she muttered, and drew her handkerchief out of her cardigan pocket.

With a woman of her type it is difficult to know whether such an action is due to hayfever, catarrh, or tears.

As I closed the door, I could not help thinking of Signor Bardoni's words, "Let her be, Mr. Compton, let her be!" In his case, the words had been accompanied by a remark about the dead hitting back, a blatant appeal to superstition. Constance Brett's stumbling appeal had been to the heart.

Both were directed to the same end.

The following is a brief record of my interview with Mrs. (Caroline) Gray, as written on the evening of October 8th:

Interviewed Mrs. (Caroline) Gray this afternoon in hotel garden, on bench. After wet morning, warm and sunny. Dahlias, some tall some dwarf, made fine colour in borders. . . .

Mrs. Gray is a dumpy woman in late sixties. Round podgy face, heavily powdered, muffin-like. Small brown eyes almost hidden by fat cheeks. Small slit for mouth. Lipstick. Sometimes seems to be sucking imaginary sweet in front of mouth. Has odd habit of repeating parts of sentences.

> *Myself:* The manageress tells me you were her closest friend in the hotel.
> *Mrs. G.:* I was, indeed I was. It is a great shock to me, a very great shock. She was a very remarkable woman. I said she was a very remarkable woman.
> *Myself:* Why was she remarkable?
> *Mrs. G.:* She just was. Everybody agreed about that. What are you writing in that notebook?
> *Myself:* Just a few shorthand notes.
> *Mrs. G.:* Why?
> *Myself:* I have a bad memory.
> *Mrs. G.:* The ways of the Lord are strange.
> *Myself:* I beg your pardon?

Mrs. G.: Her father lost a great deal of money to a crook. Her husband was in the Army. He was killed a couple of years after they were married.

Myself: In what war?

Mrs. G.: In no war. He was killed by a burglar. I said he was killed by a burglar.

Myself: By a burglar?

Mrs. G.: He went down and disturbed a burglar, and was killed. And now this awful tragedy. Strange, the ways of the Lord. Some families seem to attract trouble. I said they seem to attract trouble, some families.

Myself: It sometimes looks like it. Who were these people called the Stepping Stones?

Mrs. G.: What people called the Stepping Stones?

Myself: Well, I don't know. That's why I am asking you.

Mrs. G.: I don't wish to go on talking to you, if you are going to be rude.

(N.B. It was certainly a rude remark. But she had begun to irritate me. She was twittery and nervous, her little currant eyes were fixed on my face to note the impression she was making. Her voice took on a tone like a schoolmistress or a prison wardress. Some of these cosy-looking, muffiny-faced old ladies can be proper Tartars.)

Myself: I apologise, if I sounded rude. I did not mean to.

Mrs. G.: Very well, then. Everybody can be misunderstood. I said everybody can be misunderstood.

Myself: Quite.

(N.B. A fairly long silence. Decided to try again.)

About this Stepping Stones business, Mrs. Gray, you were her best friend, surely you—?

Mrs. G.: I didn't say I was her best friend. I was her best friend in the hotel. That's different, isn't it?

Myself: Well, do you know of any other close friends not in the hotel?

Mrs. G.: No. No, I don't.

Myself: Had your friend Mrs. Dawson any eccentric habits?

Mrs. G.: No, of course she hadn't! She was a perfectly normal woman, perfectly normal.

Myself: You said she was a very remarkable woman. So she was normal but remarkable, is that it?

(N.B. She was chewing imaginary sweet rapidly.)

Mrs. G.: Why are you trying to trip me up? Like a lawyer or a detective or something?

Myself: That's what I am—a detective or something, as you call it. I am a writer. I am going to record her case. I need to know about her. I can't just write, "Mrs. Dawson was murdered at Pompeii on September 11th and the Italian police have so far made no noticeable headway." Presumably the Stepping Stones, whoever they are, knew her well, since they sent a wreath—the only wreath, incidentally "in memory of happier times," as they put it.

Mrs. G.: Well, I cannot help you further, I must go indoors, I said I must go indoors now.

Myself: You have helped me already, thank you. You have told me she suffered twice at the hands of criminals. Now she had suffered a third time. It is a remarkable story.

Mrs. G.: No good is served by recalling tragedy. Why not let poor Mrs. Dawson rest in peace? I said, why not—

Myself: I know what you said. Two people have said the same thing already.

Mrs. G.: Then why not have the decency to heed them, Mr. Compton?

Myself: I am not convinced that she is resting in peace. On the other hand I am conscious of deliberate obstruction. I do not know why, and I cannot describe it, but I feel it. I am an old newspaper man, and senseless obstruction makes me obstinate. I am going to do a most exhaustive study of her and her past life, the tragedies in it, and her own awful end.

(N.B. I thought, mistakenly, that I had nothing to lose by being outspoken; nor had I any scruples. The hard insulting voice issuing from the pale muffiny face made me feel that this dumpy old bag merited no more courtesy than she gave, which was little or none.)

Mrs. G.: I shall now go indoors and rest for an hour before dinner, Mr. Compton, since your mind seems made up.

Myself: Two points before you go. Had she any special interests? How did she spend her days?

Mrs. G.: She spent her time like most of us do—going for short walks, talking, looking at television, and reading.

Myself: Had she many friends outside those in this hotel?

Mrs. G.: Hardly any. Probably none.

She got up and crossed the lawn to the hotel side entrance. Slow, deliberate steps. Thick ankles. Slightly bandylegged.

Illness is an operational hazard when seeking information in these hotels. I had to wait two days before a stomach upset which had befallen Mrs. Dacey allowed her to come down from her room. She was a very elegant old doll indeed. She looked about eighty, to judge from the texture of her skin. But she was slim, beautifully dressed in a plain black dress, with a simple patent leather belt, and wore elegant shoes, probably Italian. Her hair was dyed blonde, yet this, so blatantly artificial, looked decorative rather than incongruous.

She was the widow of a minor diplomat, and in the course of

our conversation she told me quite frankly that she spent her time reading biographies and historical works, playing patience, and waiting for death. She was coolly philosophical.

I enjoyed talking to her, and in this sense the delay was worthwhile. It is always pleasing to meet somebody who is determined to be elegant, intelligent, and unperturbed, right to the end of the road. Such people think they are no longer of use to the world. They are wrong. They are no longer leaders, they are no longer even tillers of the soil, but they provide nourishment for those who come within their range, and thus, so long as their spirit holds firm, their life is worthwhile.

In all other ways, except one, Mrs. Dacey was a disappointment. She could fill in very little of the picture of Mrs. Dawson which I was trying to visualise. But she gave me four snippets of information which I noted as of possible use.

First, she said that, as in Italy, so at the Bower Hotel, Mrs. Dawson paid her hotel bill direct to the hotel manageress, an eccentricity which neither Miss Brett nor Mrs. Gray had mentioned.

Secondly, she said that Mrs. Dawson always spent a holiday abroad: not always in Italy, occasionally in France or Switzerland, or Holland, or some other country.

Third, her life, though aimless as described by Mrs. Gray, was not entirely so, since she was interested in the International Seamen's Widows and Orphans Fund; in connection with this she wrote and received a fair amount of mail, and made occasional trips to London. She knew this because Mrs. Dawson had said so herself, though reluctantly, not wishing her charitable activities to be widely known.

Four, Mrs. Dawson's friendship with Mrs. Gray was such that Mrs. Gray was to all intents and purposes her devoted slave. She helped her to undress at night, and dress in the morning, she brushed her hair, packed when Mrs. Dawson went away, unpacked when she returned, and waited on her hand and foot.

This I found extraordinary.

This fascinated me more than anything I had yet heard.

Caroline Gray was an unpleasant old bag, physically and mentally tough, unsentimental, unyielding, and self-sufficient.

If Mrs. Gray was like that, and Lucy Dawson could dominate her, what did that make Lucy Dawson beneath her gentle frail exterior?

I could find no answer to the question before I left the Bower Hotel.

CHAPTER 3

On the evening of October 10th, I caught the 8.25 p.m. train back to London. It was cold, it had been bitterly cold all day. Suddenly, unexpectedly, the first touch of winter had descended, and with it a thick mist.

Either the heating on the train had gone wrong, or they had forgotten to switch it on, and I sat huddled in a corner of the carriage, sometimes thinking, sometimes trying to doze, waiting for the train to gather speed, which it never did.

Opposite me a woman sat, large and ungainly, her figure shrouded in a thick jersey and a short coat, topped off with a white mackintosh. She looked about fifty, and had a round face encased in a layer of wool, a cross between a skiing hat and a blue child's bonnet, which tied under the chin. Myopic, naïve eyes looked through large horn-rimmed spectacles; mostly at the mist-covered night, sometimes at me.

I guessed she wanted to talk, and took no notice. I dislike talking on trains. And I was thinking about the Bower Hotel.

The visit had not been an entire success, but at least I had seen the place where Lucy Dawson had lived. I could write:

> *Old Mrs. Dawson, who was murdered in Pompeii, was a woman in her late seventies. A tall, thin, frail woman, she lived most of the year at the Bower Hotel, Burlington-on-Sea, a good class residential hotel. She liked to spend a few weeks on the continent each year.*
>
> *For the rest of the time, her life appeared to be uneventful, mostly whiling away the days in the manner usual in such hotels, though she took some interest in a seamen's charity.*
>
> *Tragedy, however, was already known in her family. Apart from the fact that her father lost most of his money as a result of a business transaction with crooks, her husband had been murdered after only two years of marriage when he disturbed a burglar; and now she herself was destined to die a tragic death behind the sunbaked walls of an ancient Roman city.*

I leaned my head against the train upholstery, eyes closed, forming the dull, uninspired sentences in my mind as the train ground its way through the mist.

As a background picture it was terribly thin, but it was the best I could do at the moment.

As to the Stepping Stones, who had sent a wreath, I was beginning to lose interest in them. The wording, "In memory of happier times," was old fashioned and pedantic. They were possibly some amateur entertainment group with whom Lucy Dawson had once been associated, two or three of whom still survived in London or some provincial town. Perhaps they even met from time to time to play a piano and entertain each other in reedy voices with songs from their youth.

I was beginning to paint a sentimental picture of them, when suddenly, to my annoyance, the woman opposite me spoke.

"The fog service is always much worse on Sundays."

"Yes," I said, hating her, and opened my eyes, and closed them again.

"Still," the voice went on, "I'm well wrapped up and I quite enjoyed a day in the country."

The word "quite" sounded a sad little word, indicating that the speaker had not enjoyed her day in the country as much as she had expected. I sighed.

"Hardly a day to plod round the woods," I said, since what had to be had to be. "It's not exactly primrose weather."

"No," she said solemnly, "it's not the right time of year for primroses. I missed Mass, too."

"You are a Catholic, I suppose."

"Yes, are you?" she asked eagerly.

I am not a Catholic, but Juliet is, and I know a good deal about the subject. Suddenly, I saw myself engaged in some ghastly Protestant v. Catholic argument, of the kind which invariably leads nowhere at all. This I could not contemplate.

"Yes," I said, to forestall it.

"And I suppose you *practise?*"

"Oh, yes," I said, in case she should start giving me a tolerant lecture about overcoming the Weaknesses of the Flesh. I need not have worried.

There was a pause. Then she said:

"I was brought up by the nuns. I would like to have gone to Mass today, but I couldn't find a church. I remember when I made my first Communion. I wore a white veil and lilies of the valley."

She seemed to droop. A dreadful feeling of nostalgia, as damp as the fog, emanated from her and I gave a mental groan. I was not in the mood for childhood reminiscences, and I didn't want to feel sorry for her. There is a glutinous monotony about youthful innocence lost.

I said nothing.

She took a grubby handkerchief from her pocket and blew her nose, and looked like a female counterpart of a schoolmaster who had taught me chemistry, and to whom we boys had been very cruel. I hoped, too, that the conversation was at an end, and to help its closure I shut my eyes again.

After a while I half opened them cautiously.

Her own eyes were swimming with tears, and she was wiping them with a grubby handkerchief.

I am a sucker for adult tears, because although they embarrass me they expose the helplessness and childishness which does not lie so very deep in people. She said:

"I'm terribly sorry, but I can't stop crying."

"Well, never mind," I said, which must rank among the top, winning lines for fatuity. She began to sob now.

"I've lost a very great friend. Do you believe in life after death, do you think we survive?"

"Of course I believe in it," I said stoutly.

"I don't want the obvious answers," she said, but with no echo of reproof. "I mean, do *you* believe it?"

"Yes, I do. If one doesn't believe that, there is no point to life. You might as well put your head in a gas oven," I added, and regretted the words as soon as I had spoken them.

"That's what I'm afraid of," she said flatly.

There is a horrid quiet grimness at suddenly looking at a human soul when it has reached the pit of darkness. You grope around tongue-tied. There's the wind on the heath, brother, and grief passes in the end, and all the other hackneyed stuff, but you know it won't do. She sat looking at me like a dog in an anti-vivisection advertisement.

The seconds passed.

"Despair is a terrible thing," I said. God Almighty, one had to say something.

She began to wipe her eyes again.

"You should try not to give way," I added hopelessly.

We went through a tunnel, and the lights, for some obscure reason known only to British Railways, promptly went out.

In the damp darkness I could hear muffled sniffs, and small movements like a rabbit in a hutch. When the train rattled its way out of the tunnel the lights came on, and I saw she had struggled out of her mackintosh and taken off her head covering. She wore a man's collar and tie, and her grizzled hair was cut rather close to her head. She blinked and said:

"Of course, I do realise it's partly my fault, but it's terrible when you have two people in love with you."

I gazed at the fantastic plainness of her face, noting a certain bun-faced honesty, and wished angrily that she had looked evil. She said:

"My friend who died was older than me, and the friend who is living with me is young. The young are hard. They don't understand. I can't even cry, except in the toilet."

"Why won't she let you cry?"

"She's an atheist, she doesn't want me to take up God again. She says it's weak-minded. She won't have a lot of mumbo-jumbo, she says. But it's terribly hard, terribly hard."

The tears began to drip from her eyes once more, but she did not mop at them. Her body did not move. She just apologised again.

"What about your work?" I muttered. "I suppose you do work?"

"Yes, I work for an Adoption society."

I sighed with relief, glad of any straw to help me out of a feeling of utter inadequacy, and said:

"Well, there you are—there's your scope for the future—helping to provide a happy future for—"

But she wouldn't let me finish.

"I know all that, I was enthusiastic at one time, but some of those people are so cynical. Do you know what one of them said to me last week, rubbing her hands together? 'Christmas will soon be here,' she said, 'they'll all be having a drink or two too many, and then by September we shall have a good many new babies to place.' I think it's disgusting. I mean they're not replacements, they're people, small people, anyway," she concluded awkwardly.

"That's right," I said, and glanced at my watch. "We'll be in at Victoria Station in a few minutes," I added, but it wasn't any good.

"She was very good to me, my friend who died. I'd like to see her again. It would be nice to explain."

"You'll see her again," I said dully.

People often think that explanations can change things, can soften the blow of adultery, smooth over the loss of love, pour oil on the surface of life; and the seas will abate, and all will be as it should be. It's bunk.

"She was much older than me, I told you that. We still went on being friends after. She wasn't bitter. I'm sure she understood."

I nodded. There was nothing I could say which was worth saying.

"She said she'd leave me £100 in Premium Bonds. That shows she still cared, don't you think? Do you think I ought to practise my religion again?"

"It's something you've got to decide for yourself," I replied, and knew she wanted me to go through the motion of deciding for her.

"I suppose so." Her voice was grief stricken. "Do you know, her family didn't even invite me to the funeral. You'd think they'd have had the decency to do that, wouldn't you? Some people! They said it was because I was a Catholic."

Her eyes took on an expression of stubborn indignation.

"That was just an excuse. They knew perfectly well I hadn't been to church for years. What harm would it have done letting me go to church to pay my last respects? Still, I went, just to spite them. What is more I walked the way to the cemetery afterwards, carrying my wreath. I owed it to her. So it was all right in the end, wasn't it?"

"You did the right thing," I said, and my voice sounded like an echo of futility itself.

"That's what I thought. It helps when you know you've done the right thing."

"Oh, yes it does."

The train was slowing down in Victoria Station. I could hardly wait for it to stop. She was heaving herself into her silly white mackintosh, adjusting her ludicrous head covering. I heard her murmur something about catching a No. 52 bus, and saw her open a big shabby handbag, and take out a buff-coloured envelope. Suddenly, impulsively, I blurted out:

"Don't do anything foolish. Suicide is no solution."

The train had almost stopped. She said:

"You may be right. But it's hard to go on."

"Try."

She nodded. Then she swallowed, and sought the same old assurance.

"I shall see her again?"

"Of course, of course you will," I said, and reached thankfully for the door handle as the train stopped.

We walked a little way along the station platform together.

"She left me a barometer, too. I do hope I get it. But the family are making a fuss."

I indicated a side entrance, and said I'd have to take a taxi as I was late. I wasn't. I had nothing to be late for, but I wanted to get back to normality and away from sadness. I felt I couldn't stand it any longer. I could have given her a lift part of the way, but I couldn't stand it, not any longer.

Yet at the last moment she detained me with a red, square, hand laid on my arm, and said:

"It's been such a help talking to you. It's not often you find somebody who understands. These days everyone is so hard. They don't seem to understand the nice things in life."

I felt ashamed by her simplicity, and appalled by the memory of my inability to offer real comfort. I shook my head and began to mutter something, but she interrupted me and said:

"Because you've been a help to me, here is something which may help *you*. I do hope it will. I really do. But don't read it till you're back home."

She thrust into my hands the buff-coloured envelope she had taken from her handbag, and left me, and her squat figure hurried on in the direction of the main station entrance.

I have described the incident at some length because I believe that despite the hold which certain people had on her, her sorrow and grief were sincere.

I believe she thought the small role she played to be innocuous, as indeed it was. Whether she had performed less innocuous acts in the past must be a matter for speculation. On this occasion I am certain she was not play-acting, because it would have been pointless to go to such lengths.

Actually, I thought the buff envelope probably contained some extract from the Bible or something, and I put it in my pocket, had a couple of drinks at the Devonshire Arms near my flat and forgot all about it till I was undressing.

When I opened it, it contained an ordinary quarto sheet of white paper, on which was typed the following:

> *Investigations into the background and death of Mrs. Dawson at Pompeii are a matter for the Italian police and nobody else. Investigation by other persons can only be regarded as unwarranted intrusions.*
>
> *It is hoped and believed that you will appreciate this point, particularly since it is understood that you contemplate marriage in a month's time.*

There was no signature.

Feelings merge, and blend, and overlap, and it is hard to sort them afterwards, but I think I can truthfully say that the thing which first impressed me, as much as the cumbersome threat, was the appalling heaviness of the phraseology, the awful resemblance to the style used by lawyers and civil servants.

Then I read it through again, and noted how the capital letter "I" was defective, and reproduced itself with the lower part missing, and how the "e" and the "o" were blurred and clogged, and I glanced at my own typewriter on the desk by the window, and remembered that for some time it had required overhaul, and cleaning, and repairs to the letter "I"; and when I held the paper up to the light and saw the watermark, "64 MILL BOND EXTRA STRONG," I hardly needed to look at the watermark on my own paper on the desk, or at the buff envelopes I keep in the letter rack.

It is all very fine to see these things on the films or television, but when they happen to you personally you experience the feeling you get when you completely mislay something you have seen only a few minutes ago. You wonder if you are going mad, or are in a dream, or even dead.

I stood still with a singing sound in my head, and this was mingled with the thumping noise of my heart, and with vague distant sounds of people laughing and talking loudly, and the sound of cars starting, which showed that the tavern down the road had shut.

After about two minutes, I heard the faint creak of a floor board from the spare bedroom which Juliet and I were turning into a dining-room. The door was closed.

I went into the hall and fetched a knobkerrie given me by an uncle. For those who do not know, in these post-Imperial times, a knobkerrie is a wooden stick with a large heavy knob, formerly much used by African natives. It could be flung through the air, or used as a club in battle, or for polishing off wounded warriors after battle. Its modern uses are limited.

It gives a psychological reassurance when faced with a closed door, but that is about all. I opened the door a couple of inches, groped, switched on the light, flung the door wide, and felt a fool.

There was nobody in the flat. Nothing had been disturbed. More particularly, when I examined the front door, there were no scratches round the Yale-type lock or round the paintwork on the door or windows.

I went to bed, tense, worried, and listening.

The attempts in Italy and England to dissuade me from probing into the case had till now seemed isolated incidents, reasonably civilised, and explainable on one pretext or another.

Tonight's affair was different.

Although I had not the slightest intention of abandoning my plans, I was, I admit, getting jumpy. If somebody had been in my flat once, they could come into it again.

I record that I lay in bed in a very uneasy mood, thinking of Bardoni, Miss Brett, Mrs. Gray, that thick-set, muffin-faced old Tartar, and the sad, sad woman in the train and the message she had given me.

I had spoken to Mrs. Gray of senseless obstruction. There was obstruction all right, no longer negative but positive, and it could not be senseless. But what was behind it was as unclear as ever, and why they had gone to the trouble of entering my flat illegally and using my typewriter and paper baffled me.

At first I thought it was an attempt to gain their ends by melodrama, but I abandoned that line. It now seemed part of a detailed operation planned to overcome any stubbornness on my part. I noted that now, for the first time, I was thinking in terms of They and Them.

For the first time, too, the peasant realised he had caught a clear sight of green eyes, heard the sound of feline bodies, and the cracking of twigs, and become properly conscious of jungle peril.

It was unpleasant but it was not yet terrifying.

At one-thirty in the morning I was still awake. I got up, warmed some milk, poured an enormous slug of whisky into it, took two aspirins, and went back to bed. In fifteen minutes I was sound asleep, which is not surprising. Anyway, peasants usually sleep well.

I decided I would call in at the police station first thing in the morning, and fell asleep trying to think what I would say.

I need not have worried. I had a call myself, first thing in the morning.

CHAPTER 4

At about six-thirty in the morning I was awakened by the sound of a car changing gear noisily and accelerating. An electric trolley hummed past, bottles clinking, to start a milk round. I did not think I would fall asleep again. I was out of routine.

It was light in the living-room but not in the kitchen. I switched the kitchen light on, made a pot of tea, carried it over to my desk and lit a cigarette.

When the 'phone rang at six-fifty, I realised it was early morning in Washington, about one-fifty by Juliet's time. I felt sure it was Juliet ringing on her return from some farewell party.

The day was grey. I was eager to hear her voice. But as I moved to the telephone a depressing thought occurred to me. She would be due to leave soon. Would she be telephoning unless it was to say that her return had been delayed? I lifted the receiver.

"Mr. James Compton?"

I thought it was a personal call. So it was, in a way.

"Speaking."

"I take it you got the note last night?"

It was a man's voice: cultured, low pitched, rather pleasant.

"What note?"

I wanted time to think. I felt mentally numb.

"A note delivered by hand to you."

"Oh, that," I said.

"Yes, that. You're up early. I saw your light go on."

"Look," I shouted, "I don't give a bloody damn who you are, or what the idea is, but you can stop your bloody silly tricks!"

You could say that the numbness was wearing off.

"Listen to me."

"I've no intention of listening to you."

"I should, if I were you."

"I'm not you," I said, and regretted the schoolboy retort. Stratford Road is narrow, and outside I could hear two lorry drivers calling to each other.

"Hello?" I said, after some seconds.

"Don't worry, I'm still here," he said.

"I don't give a damn if you're there or not."

"Then why are you hanging on the line?"

I slammed the receiver down, stared at it for a few seconds, and walked over to the tea tray. I swallowed some tea.

When the 'phone rang again, I put the cup down and went over and lifted the receiver. I was quite calm now.

"We got cut off," he said, in his rich, imperturbable voice.

"Yes, I cut us off," I said.

"I thought it was the operator. The service is so bad these days."

"The service isn't so bad. And it wasn't the operator."

I suppose he didn't expect a counter-attack. I think he was accustomed to dealing with people who crumpled quickly. After a few moments he said:

"Hello? Mr. Compton?"

"Don't worry. I'm still here," I said, repeating his phrase.

"I don't care if you are or not," he said.

"Then why are you ringing again?"

"I think we ought to get down to brass tacks," he said.

"Yes, do—do so now. I'm bored."

"You're not."

"Let's stop it," I said. "Let's assume *you've* been successful in this psychological warfare nonsense."

"I have been successful," he said.

"Good old you! Now what?"

"Now nothing."

"Nothing?" I said. "What do you mean, nothing?"

"Nothing in regard to Lucy Dawson. From you or by you. That's all."

In an odd way I was enjoying the exchanges. I felt keyed up, alert, and this was at least a human contact, with whom I could get to grips.

"Are you a crook?" I asked pleasantly. "Are you a crook by any chance?"

"Sometimes yes, sometimes no. Like most of the citizenry. Are you God? Why hasten the Day of Resurrection? Mrs. Dawson needs no flesh and blood from your hands."

"You're the fourth person who has been on at me about this. Fifth, if you count that miserable woman in the train."

"What woman in what train?"

"The one who gave me the note."

"I thought it arrived by carrier pigeon."

He gave a whinnying laugh. It sounded like a green woodpecker and contrasted with his well-modulated voice.

"That's not funny," I said. "It's corny."

"Not funny. Not corny. Evasive."

"Mrs. Dawson can't betray you," I said. "She's dumb for ever. What's the matter with you? What are you afraid of? Who are you? Not that you'll tell me, not that I expect you to tell me, I'm just keeping the social chit-chat going, Buster."

"My name's not Buster."

"Surprise, surprise. Who are you? Not that I'll believe you."

"I am seven, like the devils in the Bible—seventeen or seventy—or seven hundred. Anything you choose, really."

"Good luck to you all."

"And you are one," he murmured. "How much do you hope to make out of the story? Five hundred pounds? A thousand?"

"That's not on," I said.

"Used one-pound notes?"

"We aren't speaking the same language."

There was silence. After about five seconds he asked:

"What language *are* you speaking? How much?"

"I might have got fed up with the case," I said, "if you hadn't been so silly, all seven hundred of you. Now it's a matter of principles."

I heard a groan come over the 'phone.

"Dear God, dear God! A matter of principles! Poor, poor old hackneyed phrase! Last refuge of the obstinate who've run out of arguments, final defence of the dull witted, end of the line of reason. When our flanks crumble and our centre caves in, and the trumpets sound Retreat, what do we do but fall back on that last massive, mossy, hoary old citadel?"

"Well delivered, but too many similes and analogies. Any other prepared speech by you?"

He reverted to ordinary conversational tones:

"Well, it's been nice talking to you."

I heard a click and guessed he had replaced the receiver.

"Hello?" I said. "Hello?"

"Did you think I'd hung up?" He gave another of his green woodpecker laughs. "I was just pretending, like when one's a dear little child. A d-e-e little, innocent little child. Did you used to play 'Let's pretend' when you were a dee little, innocent little child? I bet you did, Jamie, boy. I bet you're still a dee innocent little child at heart. Let's pretend now."

"You're barmy. Mad," I said, and meant it.

"Not barmy. Not mad. Cool, clear brain."

"They all say that."

"We all say that," he agreed cheerfully. "My friends and I, we all say that. Cool, clear brains, we say. So let's pretend."

I had had enough. I wanted to be clear of him. There was nothing to be got out of this nonsense. He was a voice, only a voice, and would remain a voice.

"I'm going to report it to the police," I said.

"Report *what* to the police?" he asked sadly.

"That message, typed on my typewriter, and my paper. And this 'phone call."

"Oh, that. Yes, of course you will. Who wouldn't? So let's pretend."

When I switched the telephone receiver from one hand to another I saw that it was glistening, and yet I didn't replace the receiver on its cradle. I guessed that if I did the telephone bell would ring again soon, and if it didn't ring, I would wish that it had done. One part of my mind tried to tell me he was unbalanced. But I knew he wasn't, at heart I knew he wasn't.

"Pretend what?"

"Pretend that you agree to drop the Lucy Dawson story."

"I have no intention of dropping it."

"I said, let's pretend. So you drop the idea—as from now. So what happens? You're in the clear. You're happy and free to go ahead with your wedding and live happily ever after. Comparatively prosperous, and comparatively respected by all who know you. Right?"

"Not right," I muttered. "Not respected by all who know me."

"Who wouldn't respect you?"

"I wouldn't respect me."

"Final?"

"Final," I said, "unless you explain things more."

There was another click, and this time I knew it meant the end of the conversation. I replaced the receiver and sat staring at the window. I keep a small bowl of water there for pigeons. I like all birds, even pigeons, which are supposed to be so destructive. A pigeon landed, bedraggled and dirty white, and strutted towards the bowl, flicking its head from side to side, looking for danger, knowing danger was around, but not knowing where.

I didn't like the silence in the flat. I wished the telephone conversation was still going on. While I could hear the voice, even with its sneers, I knew I could cope, because I was in touch with whatever was afoot; intangibly, even negatively, but at least in touch.

Now there was only the interior quietness of the flat.

Somebody knew my movements, almost from hour to hour. He knew the train I would catch from Burlington, and had seen the light go on in my kitchen, when I got up to make tea.

We are seven, he had said, or seventeen, or seventy, or seven hundred, and you are one. I walked over to the window, and the white bedraggled pigeon flew off and settled on a roof guttering on the opposite side of the street.

I looked down into the street. Nobody was noticeably hanging around in doorways, but then they wouldn't be. Not noticeably. Across the street it was different. Across the street there were a couple of dozen windows with curtains of different kinds, varying from heavy velvet curtains to light net curtains. All equally effective, from the point of view of concealed eyes.

It is a strange feeling standing by the window, openly, knowing that somebody is certainly watching you, not with personal interest, as a neighbour might, but with meticulous, business-like attention. Heartlessly, as the pigeon was doing.

I looked at the pigeon, and the pigeon looked at me. It was waiting for me to move away from the window before landing on the sill for a drink.

I turned and went to the bathroom and shaved and had a long bath. After I had dressed I looked at myself in the mirror as I tied my tie, and I did not much care for what I saw.

I was strongly built, admittedly, but on the short side, about five feet eight inches. Round, bullet head, due to a mixture of English, Irish and Boer blood. Crew-cut brown hair, and brown eyes. Complexion still suntanned from Italy but turning fawn. Face round, rather heavy, obstinate jaw and lower lip. Poor old Juliet, I thought.

I wasn't proud of being obstinate. Far from it. I just knew that in some matters I never had the slightest intention of deviating one iota from my intentions. One such matter was Lucy Dawson. That was the streak of Boer blood in me. The trait that got the Boers through the Great Trek, and also into a lot of grave difficulties since.

Still, it was a great trek while it lasted.

I jumped like a scalded cat when the 'phone rang again. That's my trouble, I look phlegmatic, but I'm not, I jump like that well known scalded cat sometimes. I strode over to the telephone and lifted the receiver and said loudly:

"Well, what do you want now?"

It was Stanley Bristow, my future father-in-law, ringing to confirm or amend previous engagements for that evening. He was like that, everything had to be checked at least twice.

"What's up with you, old boy?" said Stanley Bristow's snuffly little voice.

"Sorry, I thought you were somebody else."

"Who? Your bookmaker, old boy? Being dunned? Can't you pay, old boy? You can always plead the Gaming Act, old boy!"

"No, just somebody else. I'll tell you sometime. It's a long story."

"Good. And I've got a story for you, when I see you, old boy. About a coloured American soldier, and three chorus girls, one Irish, one Scotch, and one English. Remind me to tell you."

"I'll remind you. If you forget, I'll remind you," I said.

"Just a minute. The wife's gone out of the room. I can probably tell you now, if you like."

"Well, there's somebody downstairs at the door," I lied.

Some dirty jokes are funny, but not Stanley's. Never Stanley's.

"All right. I just wanted to say that I've had another thought about tonight. I don't think we'd better go by car."

"You don't?"

"No, I've booked a table at that little place in Charlotte Street. Impossible to park round there, old boy. Taxi's the only thing."

"Taxi," I repeated.

"Taxi, old boy. So you could drop Juliet here at five-thirty, after you've picked her up at the airport, then drive back to your place and change, and then either drive up here and leave your car here, or come up on foot."

"Drive up or come up on foot," I said patiently.

"It's not far to walk, as you know."

"No, it's not far to walk. I must go now."

"See you this evening, old boy."

The thought of seeing him regularly through the years was appalling. Yet one had to be gentle with him. It seemed to me that there was no malice in the man. In fact, despite the irritation he aroused in me, I felt sorry for him.

He had recently retired from the post of general manager in a small, but long established firm, which over the decades had slowly evolved from making tin and wooden children's toys to plastic ones. Stanley said that they might be old-fashioned, but they moved with the times. It was the sort of remark one might expect him to make. He also said they combined the tradition of the past with the spirit of the future. Dear me.

He had married Elaine Bristow late in life, by which time he had somehow managed to save a good deal of money, and Elaine had a little of her own. What with a small inheritance from a brother, and his pension, and his savings, and Elaine's money, they were able to live at a reasonable standard in a ground floor flat between Kensington Church Street, and Camden Hill, which is not a cheap area.

He should have been happy, but I wondered if he was.

Since his retirement, he had spent most of his time going alone to race meetings, and interesting himself in various Service benevolent organisations, which entailed visiting people and eating and drinking for charity.

It seemed to be doubtful if he was particularly interested in racing or horses or charity. He was certainly interested in getting out of the house, not that Elaine Bristow actively nagged him. She just treated him with a faint, amused contempt.

"It is, of course, difficult to make really worthwhile money these days, if one is honest like Stanley," she would say, or, "Personally, I would like to have had more than one child, but there, it was not to be."

Stanley affected to take no notice of these remarks, with their snide reflections on his financial acumen and his virility. She was a tall, over-blown woman, and she was always pleasant enough to me. I played her along on her own terms, the same as I did her husband.

Sometimes I wondered how this superficial couple could ever

have given birth to somebody like Juliet, with her intriguing, with-drawn manner, and her thoughtful, secretive glances. Both Stanley and Elaine were fair. Both had tall, substantial figures, though not actually stout. Stanley's hair was sparsely distributed over his rect-angular Anglo-Saxon skull, and was grey except for a few streaks here and there which remained tow-coloured.

Elaine Bristow's hair was fair all over, and people were allowed to draw their own conclusions about it. Both had grey eyes. Both in their different ways were seemingly extrovert types.

Out of this physically consistent nordic blending had come Juliet—of only medium height, dark-haired, pale, slim, brown-eyed, and quiet.

The thing which I noted most of all, in the beginning, was her watchfulness. She would be thumbing through a magazine, or eat-ing her meal, saying little, while her parents and I talked. Now and then, without moving her head, she would glance towards us, and if I glanced back she would drop her eyes. She wasn't consciously flirting, she was discreetly observing.

It was difficult to know whether she was secretive or shy, and I didn't care. I just knew that almost from the first moment I met her at a cocktail party I found her enchanting and wanted to marry her. I was thirty-two, no bleating lamb turned loose on the world, but Juliet was the only one who had ever aroused in me a feeling which justified the words "blind passion."

Passion it was, entirely physical at first; and blind, because al-though men of mature age will usually regard the physical side of love as a big incentive, they will seek for some other ingredients before proposing marriage, such as gaiety, wit, a sense of humour; even kindliness, though this ranks lower in the scale; nor do I think that money counts for much with men, though women think it does.

When I met Juliet, I knew I would seek for none of these things. So it was blind passion. For better or for worse. I was aware of the gamble I was taking, but I wanted the woman and, all things being equal, I was going to have her, whether I regretted it later or whether I didn't.

She wore glasses, not all the time, not at parties, or when she wished to look her best, as she thought; but when she was at the cinema or theatre, or reading, or driving a car.

Women with glasses attract me, as they attract many other men. Perhaps the greatest untruth ever spoken by a talented woman were the words of Dorothy Parker, "Men don't make passes at girls with glasses."

Men do. Hordes of them.

It's not a question of a fetish, or sex deviation. Psychologically, it's simple. Glasses indicate a physical weakness. Weakness arouses the protective instinct. Most men are suckers about being protective. It's as clean and simple as that.

Juliet, glasses or no glasses, didn't arouse any particular protective instinct in me when I met her. Her shy-sly withdrawn manner, and soft voice, and soft hands, and soft shoulder blades when we danced, they didn't arouse any Sir Galahad feelings in me, I assure you, and what feelings they did arouse don't need to be spelt out in this day and age.

I don't believe that it was Helen's face that launched a thousand ships and led to the sack of Troy. No woman's face is worth the effort. But if you said that a thousand ships were launched because Helen had a shy-sly manner, a secretive, thoughtful way of glancing up at a man, and then away again, a supple, yielding body, and a skin like a magnolia leaf, then I would believe you, whether her face was beautiful, or, like Juliet's, oval and classically undistinguished.

Let's face it. Lust caused me to gamble on Juliet.

Good fortune alone decreed that she had those other ingredients which men hope for and sometimes get and sometimes don't. So I was lucky. But I would have proposed to her anyway.

The frame of her horn-rimmed glasses was black, and perhaps too heavy for the delicacy of her face. Not that it matters at all.

It was her father's 'phone call which set me off thinking about her, in fact, all three of them, as I dressed and boiled an egg and made some toast, and prepared to call at the police station.

I never made that visit because the door bell rang just after eight-thirty. I went to the door thinking it might be a parcels delivery or even a cable from Juliet in New York saying her time of arrival had been changed. But it was a police sergeant who had apparently cycled round from Kensington Police Station. He still wore his trouser clips.

I was surprised and pleased to see him, thinking that something suspicious might have been reported by a neighbour in my absence.

He was a middle-aged man, rather short as London policemen go, and when he took his helmet off I saw that he was bald on top, with grizzled hair above the ears.

He asked me if I was Mr. James Martin Compton, and I said I was, and asked him if he would like a cup of tea. He said, no, he had just had a cup. I asked him to sit down, but he said, no, he wouldn't be very long, and he'd just as soon stand. I said:

"I am glad you called."

To which he replied:

"Then I take it you were not altogether surprised, sir?"

"Well, yes and no," I said. "The fact is I've been away for a few days, and I think—indeed, I'm sure—that somebody has been into this flat in my absence. I was going to call round at the Station and mention it. I thought they might as well know about it. Not that they can do anything about it."

He had taken a sheet of paper from his pocket while I was speaking, and when I had finished he looked up from it, and around the living-room, moving his head slowly, his big, brown, good-natured eyes seemingly searching for some intruder who might still be there.

He looked at me for a couple of seconds, and then down again at the piece of paper in his hand, and cleared his throat. He said:

"Well, we can come to that later, sir. Whatever has happened here, or has not happened here, is not the reason for my visit, sir."

I had the impression he was ill at ease.

"Meaning what?" I asked.

"Did you travel on the eight-twenty-five train last night from Burlington via Brighton to Victoria Station, sir?"

I had brought the breakfast tray into the living-room, with some tea, and toast, and the egg and the butter and marmalade. I was pouring out a cup of tea when he asked his question. I went on pouring, having no idea what was coming.

"Yes, I did."

"Did you have in your compartment a female, possibly between the age of forty-five and fifty, dressed in a white mackintosh, and wearing a head-covering, attached beneath the chin?"

I added the milk to the tea, and nodded, and carefully replaced the little milk jug on the tray. I didn't feel sick, but I felt a surge of dull pain in the stomach.

"Yes, I remember her," I said, and remembered the tears welling out of the naïve eyes, and although I also thought of the note she had given me, it was the thought of the grief I had witnessed which was uppermost in my mind.

The note, and its message, was a minor thing at that moment, a trivial, stupid little mystery compared to the major issues of the black night of the soul, of death by suicide, of my slap-happy remark about putting one's head in a gas oven, and my tongue-tied inadequacy in the face of her distraught pleas for reassurance.

I saw the significance of her longing for an assurance about life after death and about whether she would see her friend again. Inadvertently, I had taken the wrong line.

By assuring her that she and her friend would survive the grave, and that she would see her friend again, I had given her the arguments she needed, the confidence which had been in the balance, about what would happen if she took her own life. If I had told her there was no life after death, she would have fought on, struggling to maintain the Awareness, which is life, against the Dreamless Sleep, which the atheists consider to be death.

It is surprising how fast such thoughts can pass through the mind. They flash between the time it takes to lift a milk jug and pour some drops into a cup; or during the time it takes to add two lumps of sugar. One moment you are happy, or if not happy, you are at least stabilised in the general turmoil of life, and the next you are sick with guilt and with a hopeless feeling of your own inadequacy to lead and inspire.

I felt sure, and still feel sure, and always will feel sure, that her emotions were genuine, even though the sergeant now said:

"At about eleven-thirty last night, a person of the above description called at Kensington Police Station and laid a complaint against a person of your name, sir, of this address, alleging that you had made improper and indecent suggestions. She declined to give her own name and address, sir, or to make a formal statement."

He was reading from his piece of paper, so as to get the exact wording right.

"I have to inform you, sir, that in the circumstances, and failing further evidence, it is not the intention of the police to take further action. It is felt that you should nevertheless be informed of this matter, and should you wish to make any statement I am authorised to take it down."

He folded up his sheet of paper and replaced it in his tunic pocket. I could almost hear him sigh with relief. We looked at each other awkwardly, in silence.

"We get this sort of thing now and again, sir," he said, in a soothing, matter of fact tone. "I take it you completely deny the allegation, and do not consider it necessary to make a formal statement in rebuttal?"

Short of nudging me in the ribs or kicking me on the shin, he could hardly have given a broader hint. But I couldn't take the opening.

I kept thinking of the two sides of her, the shapeless bundle which was her body, the red chapped hand dabbing at the tears with a grubby handkerchief, the childish apology for her whimpers; and on the other hand, the instructions she had been given and carried out. I doubted if they meant anything to her, or if she even knew what was in the envelope, or what was going on at all, except that she was wallowing in misery.

"I had a description of her from the desk sergeant, sir. They get hallucinations at certain times of life. Dentists suffer from the same sort of accusation sometimes, sir, when they give anaesthetics. That sort of thing. Well, I'll report back now, unless you have something to say."

He picked up his helmet from a chair.

"You don't wish to make any statement, I take it, sir? Except an oral denial?"

I shook my head, but he misunderstood me, and began to put on his helmet. He thought his job was finished.

"Yes, I do want to make a statement," I said.

He looked at me and shook his head.

"You don't need to, sir, in my view of present police intentions, of which I have informed you."

I got up and walked to the window, and said:

"It's not as simple as that. This woman you called about, this woman who made a complaint about me, there's something odd going on, and I don't understand it."

He nodded in an understanding way.

"You don't need to worry, sir, like I more or less said, we get these cases now and again. If she pesters you, sir, and if she goes on pestering you, and becomes a real nuisance, you want to get a Court injunction against her. It usually works. Frightens some sense into 'em, as it were."

He began to move towards the door again.

"It's not as simple as that," I said again. "It's difficult to explain. I travelled down with her and listened to a lot of emotional trouble, and she talked of suicide."

"A bit unstable mentally, I suppose, like they thought down at the police station, between you and me. I mean, she wasn't no beauty, I'm told, and directly I saw you, and this flat, if I may say so, I thought 'Well, if he wanted to start any nonsense like that he would choose something a bit different from her.' Not that you can always tell, of course."

He had reached the door and had his hand on the door knob. He had a fixed idea of how things were, and he wasn't interested, and I felt I had to talk rapidly to detain him.

"She gave me a note in a buff envelope. Just before we parted in Victoria Station. I want to show it to you. There's a very odd thing about it."

I picked up the note on my desk, and he came over reluctantly.

"You don't want to give your name and address to odd people

you meet on trains, if I may say so, sir, not if they seem a bit
cranky. It always leads to trouble of some sort. I suppose you felt
sorry for her."

I handed him the note, and said:

"I didn't give her my name and address—that's another point I
might mention. But read that, and then I'll tell you about it."

He stood by the window, holding the note a long way from his
face, as long-sighted middle-aged people do when they can't be
bothered to get out their spectacles, and when the telephone rang I
left him frowning down at it.

It was Juliet's father, again, confirming that I was going to meet
her at the airport at four-thirty that afternoon, and not at the air
terminal. I listened to the man's snuffly voice droning on about the
evening's arrangements.

"So you'll be back here about six o'clock, old man?"

"That's right, squire," I said.

"Then we'll go straight out to dinner, after a drink, old boy?"

"Splendid."

"Look forward to seeing you, old boy."

"Me too," I said.

He always called me "old boy." He tagged it on at the end of almost every sentence he spoke to me.

"That was my future father-in-law," I said, as I put the receiver
down. "He doesn't like leaving things to chance. He's a great orga-
niser. He'll tell you so himself, if you ask him, or even if you don't
ask him."

I didn't think the remark witty, but I thought it merited a polite smile. However, he didn't smile.

"This note you've shown me," he said. I could detect the awakened interest in his voice. "This note you said she gave you, sir. I've
been looking at the type and I happened to glance at the type of
this bit of writing you've left in your typewriter, and at the typing
paper."

I nodded eagerly.

"That's right. It's the same. So is the typing paper, and so is the
envelope. That's what I wanted to tell you."

"What did you want to tell me, sir?"

"That the note she gave me was typed on my machine, and on my typing paper, and put into one of my envelopes."

He looked at me, puzzled, trying to sort out the implications.

"That's what's so odd," I added.

"This message you typed," he began, but I cut him short.

"I don't think you quite understand what I'm getting at. I didn't type it."

"You didn't say that when you gave it to me to read, sir."

"I was going to but the 'phone rang."

He picked up the piece of paper again, and glanced at my typewriter again, because I think he felt he ought to do something. He said gloomily:

"Well, I don't know what you're getting at, sir. Are you suggesting that this lady who complained about you somehow got into this flat, got hold of your name and address, typed this stuff out, took it all the way down to the seaside, came up in the train with you, then gave it to you at Victoria Station, and then came and complained about you at the police station? Is that what you're trying to say?"

"Well, not necessarily."

"What do you mean, not necessarily, sir?"

"What I say, not necessarily. Maybe she did get into this flat and maybe she didn't. Personally, I don't think she did."

"Then who are you suggesting did, sir?"

"I don't know."

"You don't know?"

"No, I don't know—that's the point."

The thing was beginning to resemble a bad cross-talk act.

I was getting irritated, and he saw it, and that is bad when you are dealing with the police. He passed his tongue over his lips and said:

"There's no need to get annoyed, sir. You raised this matter, I didn't."

"I'm not getting annoyed."

"We were quite content to take your word in this other matter against hers—failing independent evidence, and in view of other circumstances. There was no call to show me this piece of paper."

In effect, he was telling me that he thought I had faked the whole thing in order, in some obscure way, to discredit the woman.

"Of course there was a reason to show you the paper!" I insisted loudly. "It shows that some unauthorised person has been into this flat. If that's not a matter for the police, perhaps you'll tell me what is?"

He stiffened, but to do him credit he kept his temper. Police get accustomed to dealing with excited citizens.

"Anything stolen, sir?" he asked mildly.

"Nothing."

"Anything disturbed—contents of drawers on the floor, cupboard doors open, anything like that, sir?"

I shook my head.

"Any signs of a forcible entry by the door or windows?"

"No."

"Anybody have a key of the flat apart from yourself, sir?"

"Only the woman who cleans the flat—and she wouldn't write that pompous sort of stuff, why should she? And my fiancée, she's got a key, but if you want an alibi for her, she's been in America for a month."

"This Mrs. Dawson mentioned in the note, was she known to your daily woman or to your fiancée?"

"Of course she wasn't."

"I was only asking, sir."

"Yes, well, she wasn't."

"That's all right then," he said in the patient tone of one who was not only keeping his temper but wanted you to realise it. "Who is this Mrs. Dawson, anyway?"

"She was murdered in Italy recently."

"Murdered, was she?"

"It was in the papers at the time."

"I don't read the newspapers much—except the football pages. Was she a friend of yours?"

"No, she wasn't. But I'm preparing something about the case. I write crime articles and crime novels. I've been trying to find out something about her background, and it's been hard work. I've had the idea that people have been trying to obstruct me, but it was just an idea. Now comes this note. So I was right."

"Who would try to obstruct you, sir, as you call it?"

"I don't know. That's the point, I don't know who—or why. And another thing—somebody unknown to me rang me up early this morning and asked if I'd got that note, and then tried to badger me along the same lines."

"I see, sir."

He looked down at his blue helmet, and began to polish the badge with his right thumb. Then he said:

"You write what you call crime novels—thrillers, as it were, mystery stories?"

"Yes, I do."

I saw what was in his mind. He had changed his ground, or at least extended it. He was now fumbling towards some theory that I might have typed the note myself and created some mystery for some obscure reason connected with a thriller story. But he was too punctilious to say so. He just nodded his head thoughtfully and said, "Ah." Then he straightened himself up.

"Well, sir, in regard to the other matter, I will report that you categorically deny the accusation. In regard to the matter we have just discussed, I take it you wish me formally to report your own complaint? Or do you wish to reconsider it?"

He was offering me a let out.

I replied obstinately.

"I would like you to report it. I realise that little can be done, but I would like it reported."

"Very well, sir. I'll take this message you say was typed by some unknown intruder, and I will formally report the matter, as you wish."

He folded the paper up neatly and placed it in his notebook. He didn't sigh resignedly, but it was the loudest non-sigh I've ever heard.

"Good day, sir."

"What's your name, Sergeant?"

"Matthews, sir, Sergeant Matthews, but you don't need to worry about me not reporting what you want. That's what we're paid for, sir."

"I wasn't worrying."

"That's all right then, isn't it, sir?"

He put on his helmet and let himself out without turning round. I felt he considered me to be a disappointment, a man towards whom the Force had adopted a tolerant attitude, towards whom he, in particular, had assumed a kindly, avuncular role; a man who had invented a silly story, and persisted in it, despite a chance to retract with good grace.

I heard the street door close downstairs, and walked to the window, and saw him cycling off towards the police station.

The pigeon, which I had nicknamed Tommy the Hen, because I did not know its sex, was back on the roof guttering opposite, staring across with beady eyes.

I guessed that Tommy the Hen was not the only one observing me, but I felt some relief because I had reported matters to Sergeant Matthews. He had taken my story with about a pound of salt, but at least I had lodged it with him.

As to the sad sack in the train, whom I now thought of as Bunface, the reason for her actions completely eluded me.

Quite clearly the police were wrong in their estimate of her.

Her thoughts, conscious and subconscious, were concerned with death and self-destruction and the hereafter, not with men and sex fantasies and wishful imaginings.

She was not neurotic in the way they thought. Her grief was genuine. Therefore she had lodged a complaint because she had been ordered to do so. And yet I could swear she had liked me and had been grateful to me for listening to her woes.

I imagined her checking my name and address from some scruffy piece of paper she had been given, dragging it out of her shabby handbag, holding it with her coarse, red hands in the light of a lamp standard near the police station, peering myopically at the writing.

Then, reluctantly, and because she had to, she would have gone in, well knowing what the station sergeant would think.

Poor embarrassed Bunface, I thought, poor pathetic victim.

But whose victim?

I spent part of the day trying to work, and part of it trying to puzzle out another problem. Whoever had instructed Bunface must have known that the police would take no action. Was the complaint therefore in the nature of a feint, a vicious, probing dab in the air, such as a tiger will sometimes make with its paw?

I now thought it was. But there was more to it than that.

After a couple of gins and tonic and a sandwich for lunch I felt better, for luckily I have a sectionalised mind, and my thoughts were now on Juliet and her arrival. Indeed, I was cheerful and excited as I drove to London Airport.

But I forgot that as a secretary to the Minister she might be carrying a spare briefcase or two, and travelling with him, all the way, right back to the Ministry, with the rest of the cohort of civil servants who have to accompany Ministers when they move around these days.

So my trip to the airport was wasted. All I could do was wave, and follow in my car at a discreet distance. However, I picked her up in Whitehall in the end, and although she was deadly tired, the evening proceeded inexorably to its conclusion, as planned in all its details by Stanley Bristow.

For the first part of the evening my heart bled for poor little Juliet. Her father plied her with questions in his snuffly voice, and her mother posed supplementary questions in the energetic, bustling tones of a television interviewer. If she had answered them all, the entire confidential secrets of the Washington conferences would have been round the London clubs, and many other places, too, within forty-eight hours. But they were no match for her, tired though she was.

In the end, Stanley Bristow snuffled his way to a halt, with a plaintive protest that she never told them anything. By that time, I don't think Juliet was even listening properly. She was picking at her fish in the murky candle light of the Charlotte Street restaurant. Once or twice she looked up and caught my eye, and gave one of her secretive little half-smiles, and then looked down again.

Stanley had bought champagne to celebrate her return. He was never mean with drinks. By the middle of the meal she looked a little better. So far, I had said nothing about the woman in the train from Brighton, the message, the police visit, or the telephone call.

Now I thought I might as well do so. I was banking on a lighthearted reaction from Stanley, mellow with drink. Lighthearted it certainly was. I hoped it would set the tone for the women. He gave one of the muffled guffaws which served him for a laugh.

"Somebody's pulling your leg, old boy."

"Probably."

"Of course they are, old boy!"

"Why?"

"Why? I don't know why, old boy. Why does anybody play a practical joke. Damn silly, if you ask me, old boy."

I nodded.

"You're probably right. It's a bit elaborate, it's spread over a wide area, and I don't see the point of it, but——"

"There never is much point in a practical joke, old boy."

I felt that at any moment he was going to tell me stories of practical jokers who had dug up holes in main thoroughfares, of undergraduates who had dressed up as visiting Indian potentates and inspected guards of honour, and other tales from the hoary old repertoire of practical jokers.

"There's no end to some people's childishness," said Elaine Bristow brightly. "Even Stanley, when we were first married, used to tinker about with people's cars when they came to dinner, and remove some bit of the engine, and then while they were ringing up for help he used to sneak out and put it back again, didn't you Stanley?"

"I expect you're both right," I said quickly. "I expect it's something like that."

I felt instinctively that I had to tell them about it, in case it went on. I suppose I knew instinctively that it would go on. Now I had told them. Now I could change the subject.

"What's going to win the November Handicap?" I asked.

He looked pleased. He began to tell me, at some length, going through the merits of the main equine contenders one by one, almost leg by leg. I lit a cigarette and settled back, nodding from time to time. His wife sat back, too, bored but resigned.

Juliet was fiddling about with her coffee cup. Her skin and dark hair looked paler and more exciting, in the subdued lighting of even that mediocre Soho restaurant. She wasn't wearing her glasses.

Once or twice she looked at me without moving her head, moving her eyes only, using the shy secretive glance which hitherto had always excited me. Tonight her glance didn't excite me. Her eyes were worried. She had caught my true mood.

Juliet said she would go straight to bed when we got back to her parents' flat. The fatigue caused by the work of the Washington conference and the Atlantic flight had finally caught up with her. I would have been content to take the taxi on, back to my own flat, but Stanley insisted that I should come in for a final drink and paid off the driver.

One of Juliet's two pieces of luggage still stood in the hall, and I followed her along the passage, carrying it for her. In her bedroom, I put it down, and saw she was staggering with exhaustion and although we had hardly had a moment to ourselves since her return, I just murmured a few words and kissed her, and gave her a warm hug, and said I would see her at lunchtime next day, and made for the bedroom door.

But as I drew away from her, she caught hold of me and I turned round. I thought she wanted me to kiss her again, and was rather touched, and I did, and she didn't object, but it wasn't why she had detained me. After I had kissed her again, she looked at me, and then away, in the withdrawn manner peculiar to her, and said quietly:

"You are worried. I mean, you really are a bit, aren't you?"

"No, not really. No, I'm not worried. It's a bit bewildering, and it's all rather childish and melodramatic, and I don't understand why they don't want me to go on with this story, whoever they are. But I'm not worried, because I don't see what there is to be worried about."

"Isn't that a reason to be worried?"

I laughed and said:

"Now don't you try and scare me, darling."

"I'm not trying to scare you."

"Good."

"It's just that—these times we live in."

"What about these times?"

"One feels there's so much evil around one. So much hidden danger. You know? Bits and pieces appear in the papers. Killings and kidnappings, and inexplicable scandals, and treachery, and cold, cold hate, and those are only the bits you see, you never know where it's going to erupt next, or why it happens."

"There always have been these things."

Suddenly she started to cry. I put my arm round her. I had never seen her cry before and I didn't like it.

"Come along, darling, pop into bed, and forget these things."

"How can I forget them, when they may be touching you and me? Clawing at what may be our only chance of happiness in this life, threatening our marriage."

She dabbed her eyes with the handkerchief I offered her.

"Why not drop it, darling?" she said.

"Drop what?"

"Drop the story of Lucy Dawson."

I stared at her, feeling the obstinacy which has done me so much good and harm in life almost literally congealing my mind.

"Good God, whose side are you on?" I muttered.

She began to sob in earnest now.

"Whose side are you on?" I said again.

"Yours, darling. Ours," she whispered. "I just want to be happy, that's all."

"If I knew the reason why they want me to drop it, I might— or I might not. But I don't. So I won't."

She turned away and murmured, "Men, men."

From down the passage Stanley's snuffly voice called me. He said something about, come on you two lovebirds, it's time Juliet was in bed. Something nauseating, anyway.

I kissed her again. She did her best to respond, but her heart was not in it. I went along to the sitting room, and found Stanley alone. He said Elaine had gone to bed. I wanted to go to bed, too, but he was standing by the drinks tray, fiddling about with his cut-glass whisky decanter, and tumblers, and soda syphon. I thought he was going to say, "Well, what about a nightcap, old boy?" but he didn't. He said, "What about one for the road, old boy?" To make it worse, he said, "If you drink, don't drive—if you drive, don't drink. Well, you aren't driving, old boy."

"That's right," I said. "I'm walking back. I'll have a small one."

I lit a cigarette and sighed. He handed me a whisky.

"Tired, old boy?"

"No, not really."

I wasn't feeling particularly tired. I was just dismayed, once again, at the prospect of endless periodic drinks with Stanley, of being pinned in corners by him, of looking up at him and into his protruding watery grey eyes with their touch of ex-ophthalmic goitre, while he smoothed his sparse hair with one hand, held a glass in the other, and told me yet another feeble, smutty story.

"Well, drink up, old boy—all the best!"

I drank half the tumbler of whisky and soda without a pause.

The sooner it was finished, the sooner I could go. He was standing by the mantelpiece, his back to me, and without looking round he said:

"Look, old boy, there's something I think you should know."

His voice was as snuffly as ever, but lacked the normal light-hearted overtones.

"It's about Juliet, old boy."

CHAPTER 5

W hat about Juliet?"

"I expect she'd tell you herself, if she hasn't done so already. I suppose she hasn't?"

"Hasn't told me *what*, for heaven's sake? How do I know?" I asked, and couldn't keep the irritation out of my voice.

It was late, and I know now that subconsciously I was beginning to worry about Juliet's attitude.

"I can't tell you whether she has or whether she hasn't, unless you tell what she might or might not have told me, or be about to tell me, can I? Well, can I?"

He turned round from the mantelpiece and gawked down at me, tall and spindly, and I noticed that his tow-coloured moustache had not turned as grey as his thin hair. He looked, as he sometimes implied to other people that he was, like a former member of a crack cavalry regiment officered by rich young men, though I knew from Elaine Bristow that in fact he had been in the Pay Corps during the last war.

"Well, it's only fair you should know, old boy—in point of fact, Juliet is not really our daughter. She's an adopted child."

He looked anxiously at me, swirling his whisky in his glass. He looked really worried. I could have laughed in his face.

So far from feeling dismay, I was aware of a surge of relief that Juliet was not the result of the marriage of this uninteresting couple; and mingled with the relief, piercing through it, here and there, I began to ponder certain things, such as her dark, withdrawn attractiveness, her mixture of gaiety and seriousness, the touch of mystery about her, the occasional secretive look. Were they due to her blood or to the knowledge she had of herself? Had she, in fact, suspected the truth long before they confirmed it? An overheard remark, a hastily broken off conversation, can reveal more to a child than adults realise. Children are no fools.

None of her characteristics could have stemmed from the Bristows, and I should have known it; and even if, as I had thought, she had had some more interesting ancestor, the dull Bristow blood would have thinned it beyond hope.

"My dear Stanley, what on earth does that matter?" I said lightly, and realised that in my relief that Juliet was a full-blooded non-Bristow I had for the first time called him by his Christian name.

"I hoped you'd say that, old boy. I'd have said the same myself. I'll tell you about her parents, I'll tell you something she doesn't know herself."

"You don't need to."

"It's only fair, old boy."

He went ostentatiously to the door, opened it quietly, an inch or two, as if to make sure that nobody was coming along the passage, then closed it and walked back to the fireplace.

"Actually, I'd rather not know," I said quickly. "I'd rather not have that sort of secret between Juliet and me."

"I think you should, old boy—you see she's only half English."

He spoke in a half whisper, and looked at me as if he expected me to fall down in a dead faint.

"Half English—half Italian," he muttered. "Remember that hotel I recommended near Sorrento? Remember Signor Bardoni? That's her father. Good fellow, eh? Don't know her mother, old boy. English, but just a name—Smith, or Brown or something. Disappeared. Got it?"

I nodded. I'd got it all right. But I couldn't speak.

"And she doesn't know?"

"She knows she's an adopted child, old boy. But she doesn't know who her parents are, she doesn't know Bardoni is her father. And her father doesn't know who adopted her. That's the way these adoptions go, of course, and quite right, too, old boy, saves a lot of trouble and heartache in later years. But I found out—through a friend of a friend. You know? Made inquiries. Can't be too careful."

"And you went and stayed at the hotel a couple of years ago? You and Elaine and Juliet?"

I stared at him in amazement.

"There was no danger, old boy—Elaine knew of the relationship of course, but nobody else. Wanted to go to Italy anyway. Thought it would be an interesting experiment—you know, see what happened, call of the blood and all that stuff, see if they were attracted to each other. Do you know what happened, old boy?"

I was stuck with him for years and years. It was no good showing disapproval, no good saying that in an indefinable way I felt the whole idea repellent. He wanted me to ask, "What happened?" but I couldn't. I couldn't bring myself to give him the satisfaction. I took a sip of whisky and fumbled for a cigarette.

"Do you know what happened?" he asked again. So I had to say something in the end.

"What happened?" I said.

"Nothing! Nothing at all, old boy! We all talked to Bardoni now and again. But they didn't take any interest in each other at all. Fascinating, old boy."

"How did you know he was managing the hotel?"

"Through this adoption society chap—indirectly. They keep in touch, you know, sometimes. Just in case. You know?"

I sat looking into my whisky glass, wondering why Juliet

hadn't told me herself that she was an adopted child. She must have known it would make no difference. I wondered again if it accounted for her withdrawn manner, her secretiveness. I was aware of a feeling of hurt. I said:

"At what age did you tell her that she was an adopted child?"

"At what age? Well, at the age of twenty-two, old boy! We told her tonight—after you dropped her here in your car. While she was changing to go out. Elaine went in and told her."

"Just like that—a sort of 'Welcome home' greeting?"

I couldn't keep the bitterness out of my voice. I thought if anything was typical of this dull and unimaginative pair it was to spring this news on her just when she had arrived back tired and exhausted. I was angry, and he saw it.

He went all stiff and more snuffly than ever:

"There was no need for us to tell her—or you, old boy. I trust you realise that? In these days the birth certificate merely gives the name, date, and place of birth. But Elaine and I talked it over, old boy, and at first we were against telling her—or you—and then we said no it was not fair to you, old boy. So we told her. And very reasonable she was about the whole thing. Very reasonable."

He sounded aggrieved.

I finished my whisky and got up. It is useless to be angry with stupid people, and pointless to argue with them.

"No wonder she looked pale at dinner. I thought she was just tired."

"I think she really was just tired, old boy."

He looked at me with his protruding grey eyes, leaning droopily against the mantelpiece, stroking his thin hair, a worried expression still on his face.

It was a hopeless situation. I gave up.

"Maybe she was just tired. I expect that was mostly it."

I forced myself to smile. He brightened at once.

"Good! So now we're all in the clear, old boy?"

"That's right."

"Good-o!"

"Good-o!" I repeated, and was nearly sick. "I must be off. I'll just pop along and see if she's asleep."

Her bedside light was on, but she was asleep, and did not stir when I put my head round the door. Thus I knew that she did indeed realise that the evening's revelation would make no difference to me, and was not worried.

It could also have meant that she did not care one way or the other.

⁓

The news about Juliet had driven other things from my mind. Within a quarter of an hour there occurred something which shook me considerably, because it gave a warning of the violence which lay ahead.

It has to be remembered that I was too young to have fought in the war, and that I had lived in a peaceful and well-ordered society. I was not prepared for hazards other than the normal perils of accidents or ill health.

I had read about peasants who were observed, threatened, stalked, and finally clawed down by the jungle carnivores, but it always seemed to me that if one stuck to the safer paths one could, apart from Acts of God, reckon on physical security in this twentieth century.

I had no conception, until the very end, of what I was up against.

What happened after I had finally said good night to Stanley Bristow and closed his front door can as well be told by the statement I made to the police, at about fifteen minutes past midnight, which ran approximately as follows:

My name is James Compton, of 274 Stratford Road, Kensington, London, W.8. I am an author. At about 11.50 p.m. this evening I left the house of my fiancée, Juliet Bristow, and her parents in Jameson Street to walk home.

At the corner of Jameson Street and Kensington Place, I glanced to the right to see if the road was clear

and saw two men standing under some trees on the opposite side of Kensington Place. Kensington Place is not
very well lighted. I paid no particular attention.

I walked along Kensington Place into Church Street.
At the bottom of Church Street I crossed the road to
look into a lighted shop window. When I recrossed the
road by the traffic lights I saw two men who might have
been those I had previously seen. They turned the corner into Kensington High Street, walking very fast, and
I lost sight of them.

I proceeded along the High Street and turned left
along Wright's Lane. At the bottom of Wright's Lane I
turned right, and passed a narrow entrance which leads
to a garage. About ten yards further along the road,
which is very short, a man came around the corner and
stopped me and asked for a light for his cigarette.

He leaned forward towards my lighter and I noticed
that his right hand was in his raincoat pocket. I am
aware that this sort of approach can sometimes lead to
an attack. The street was deserted. I held my lighter
away from me, and although I saw nothing suspicious I
watched him carefully. As he leaned forward with his
cigarette in his mouth, I noticed that his eyes were not
watching the flame but appeared to be fixed on something behind me, and at the same time as I noted this I
heard a slight noise behind me.

I jumped back and to one side, and turned round.
A tall man who in my opinion had been approaching me
changed direction and passed me on the edge of the
pavement. He walked very fast, almost running, and
disappeared round the corner. He was carrying a short
object in his right hand which might have been some
sort of bludgeon.

I had with me a walking stick formed from a
knobkerrie, which is a stick with a heavy knob and is
used by African natives as a weapon. I raised this in a
defensive position when I turned round. It is possible

that in the indifferent lighting he had not noticed the nature of the object I was carrying. It is possible that the sight of it deterred him.

The other man asked me whether anything was the matter. I said no but that I was a little nervy. He thanked me and walked off towards Wright's Lane.

The tall man was about six feet in height, of normal build and had a round head with what seemed to be a crew-cut hair style, grey trousers, and a light brown knee-length mackintosh with a belt. He had turned the collar up, though it was not raining or cold. This obscured the lower part of his face. He wore no hat. His hair was brown.

The other man was about five feet seven inches tall, stockily built, and had a square face with a cleft chin. He wore a soft hat with a narrow brim. The hat had a cord round it. The tips of his striped shirt collar were fastened down with small buttons. He wore a light grey raincoat without a belt, which reached down below his knees. I think his eyes were light coloured. He had a slight foreign accent. I cannot identify the accent. Both men appeared to be in their thirties. I cannot say for certain that they were the men I had seen in Kensington Place or in Church Street. I might be able to identify them again, especially the shorter one.

"That's about it," I said, and signed the stilted, jerky statement. The bored young detective watched me. He stubbed out a cheap tipped cigarette, and leaned back in his chair.

I knew what he was thinking. I was thinking the same thing: when you got it down on paper it looked pretty thin on its own. And there was nothing anybody could do about it now.

The trouble was we had got off on the wrong footing. I went into the police station and said I wanted to report an incident which seemed to link up with something I had already reported to one of their sergeants, and the station sergeant said, "I see, sir," and showed me into an interview room. Then the young detective came in, but he wouldn't listen to me.

That was the point, he wouldn't listen.

He said, "Well, all right, sir, but first let's get an idea of the present trouble, and then we'll see, we'll see about the rest of it. Now what's the present trouble, sir?"

The point is, it sounded thin, unless you had some idea of the build-up. But he cut me short when I tried to explain. He wanted the hard facts of my present "complaint," as he called it.

So when he read through what I had written, I knew he was going to be niggly.

"What you saw in his hand might have been a torch," he said.

"That's right. It might have been."

"You say he approached you. He might have been trying to pass between the buildings and you and the other chap—on the inside of the pavement, as it were."

"He might have been. But we were well over on the inside. The easier way would have been to pass us on the outside."

"People do funny things when they're walking."

"That's right. But he was approaching me at quite a sharp angle from the pavement edge."

I saw him turning the thought over in his mind, seeking some other plausible idea.

"Maybe he also wanted a light."

"Two people without a light for their cigarettes, in the same short, deserted street, at the same time? Well, anyway, why didn't he ask for one?"

"Maybe because you were waving this knobkerrie thing in his face."

"Maybe," I said patiently.

I began to wish I hadn't gone to the police station. You have the notion that you can wander into a police station and say, "I think two chaps were going to attack me ten minutes ago, off Wright's Lane. I thought you might like to know." But it doesn't work out like that. You're lucky if you get away within the hour.

It had taken some time to hack out what he wanted me to put

on paper. The little interview room, with its glaring strip lighting, was hot, stuffy and foul with the reek of stale tobacco smoke.

"I thought I'd report the incident," I said. "We're always being told to report unusual or suspicious things to the police. So I thought I'd mention it. Particularly as there is a bit of background which you won't let me mention."

"I'm not stopping you telling me anything, sir," he said stiffly. "What else do you want to tell me?"

I was obstinate now. "It doesn't matter. I've mentioned it all already to one of your people. Just put this new report in. I'm not going over the whole story again. The reports will connect up some time, provided you have some sort of carding system. Some time they'll connect up." I added sourly, "Sooner or later they will, I expect, tomorrow or the next day, this year or next."

He began to weaken.

"You're right to report this matter, sir. It's good of you to call, sir. I'll make a note of what you've just said."

We got to our feet. He didn't mean what he said, and he knew I knew he didn't mean it, but convention was satisfied. He relaxed and smiled.

"Maybe in ten minutes time I'll be taking a statement from a tall chap in a short raincoat saying he's been threatened by a gentleman carrying a knobkerrie. That's the way it goes."

"Well, you know my address," I said, and did not smile.

I came out of the police station. A uniformed police officer was walking slowly round my car, almost audibly sniffing, as a dog will walk around another dog.

"Is this your car, sir?"

I nodded.

"I've been in the police station giving some information."

"You should have left your sidelights on, sir."

"Well, it's under a street lamp. I didn't think you had to leave sidelights on in London, anyway."

I knew what he was beating up to, but again the conventions had to be maintained.

"When a car is left on a bus route, the lights must be switched on, sir, whatever other lighting is provided in the street."

"I didn't know that," I lied wearily.

"Yes, sir. Good night."

"Good night—thank you."

He trudged heavily into the station. Probably he, too, was tired and bored. I drove round to Stratford Road.

My flat is above an ironmonger's shop. It suits me, for there is nobody above me, and the buildings on either side consist only of business premises. So when I type late at night I disturb nobody.

The flat is not much to look at from the outside, but it is all right inside, though I say it myself.

There is a large living-room, a large bedroom, and two smaller rooms; one of them I use as a study, and the other is the room Juliet proposed to use as a dining-room, thus leaving no spare bedroom for anybody to stay in, which suited me admirably.

There are one or two quite nice pieces of antique furniture, given me by my father when my mother died, and he decided to live in a Hampshire inn and spend his time fishing and, I suppose, dreaming of the past. But he only survived her two years.

He had also given me a few pieces of Georgian silver, and some fine eighteenth-century sporting prints; though as to the latter, I know that from the moment she saw them Juliet had secretly made up her mind to replace them, no doubt as tactfully as possible.

She also had one or two ideas for new colour schemes when she moved in, but she was discreet enough not to dwell too much on the subject.

Sporting prints or not, and colour schemes or not, it was a good home for a bride to come to.

One is tempted to amend that last sentence, and say that it was a good home for a bride to come to provided she could see it.

I arrived back from the police station at one o'clock, parked the car in an empty space some yards up the road, and walked to my front door and let myself in, thinking that soon the rooms would be alive with Juliet's possessions as well as mine.

I hate noise, especially abrupt noise, so I always close a door quietly. I closed the street door quietly. The blue stair carpet was before me, and I went up the stairs to the flat, weary but satisfied that up to now I had done all that I could.

About four steps from the top I stopped and stared down at the carpet, and more particularly at about half-an-inch of cigarette ash which lay there.

I stood looking down at the ash.

I never leave my flat or any other building smoking a cigarette, and I never go indoors smoking one. There is a simple explanation for this: the only thing which tastes good in the open air, to my mind, is a pipe. So I stood staring down at the ash. Then I looked up at the door of the flat. I remember noting how the polished wood and the brass knocker gleamed in the light of the stairway.

I climbed the last four steps to the flat. Outside the door I gently switched off the stairs light and listened to my heart beating.

After a while I silently lifted the flap of the letter box. The flat door opened on to a very short hallway, and beyond was the living-room. Off the living-room, to the right, was the study.

I saw nobody, and pondered how much the incident earlier in the evening must have affected my nerves. I lowered the flap of the letter box, feeling rather a fool.

There was nothing left to do now but go in.

Yet I stood listening for a few seconds, regulating my breathing, glad that Juliet could not see me. Then I fumbled in the darkness for the flat key, fingering the keys on the ring, not bothering to switch on the light again, and as I did so a faint, half-stifled cough from inside the flat stilled my movements and breathing. I told myself that noises are deceptive, especially at night, and raised the letter-box flap again.

Whoever it was, he was not in the living-room. But I could see the reflected flashes of his torch as he moved about the study.

I do not think I am more cowardly than the next man, but I may be more cautious and calculating, and possibly more imaginative. I assumed that only one man was inside the flat, and I was tempted, now that the uncertainty was over, to rush in and tackle him. But what if there were two?

Perhaps subconsciously the deciding factor was the thought of my marriage, and common prudence. I tiptoed down the stairs, softly closed the street door, and walked quickly to the telephone booths in Marloes Road. As so often, the first one I entered was out of order, the box refusing to accept a coin. The floor was littered with refuse. I do not know why these booths are so often filthy and out of order.

I swore, flung myself out of the booth and into the other one. This one was filthy, too, but when I lifted the receiver I heard the dialling tone, and thanked heaven that I had four pennies, and that the box would receive them.

I put them in, then realised that you do not need coins to dial "999." Fearful that the coins might upset the routine, I pressed button "B," recovered the coins, and then dialled "999," and got through to Scotland Yard. An impersonal voice said:

"Scotland Yard—can I help you?"

"I want to report—"

"Where are you calling from, please, sir?"

"From the 'phone booths in Marloes Road. My name is James Compton, 274 Stratford Road, Kensington."

"One minute, please, sir."

There was a pause of a few seconds. Then he said quietly, almost soothingly: "What is the trouble, sir?"

"There are intruders in my flat. Perhaps you could send somebody round," I said succinctly.

"One minute, sir."

I waited. After a short pause, the voice returned.

"We will send a police car round, sir. It should be round in about three or four minutes. Right?"

"Right."

"Now if you'll go back to your flat, and wait outside, I expect the police car will be there as soon as you are. Right?"

He spoke soothingly. He was good at his job. Nor was he far out in his calculation. The car was not there when I got back, but it arrived about two minutes later; not with a jangling of bells, as in a chase, but almost noiselessly. It must have free-wheeled the last ten or fifteen yards. It drew up at the edge of the pavement with no more sound than a faint crunch.

There were two uniformed officers, and one plain-clothes

detective. They climbed quietly out and stood in a bunch for a moment, looking up at my flat windows. Then they came over to where I stood near the doorway. The sergeant spoke quietly.

"He won't want to jump from the windows, sir. Too high. Any other way of escape round the back?"

I shook my head.

"Then we should be all right, sir. Perhaps you'll let us in."

I let them in through the street door, and switched on the light, and we all trooped up the thick blue carpet. Even though there was no way of escape, save down the stairs past us, we still moved quietly. I do not know why.

I can imagine the sort of report they wrote later:

> A thorough search of the flat revealed no trace of an intruder, nor was there any sign of a forcible entry. Occupant stated that nothing appeared to have been stolen or disturbed. In the light of these facts, it seems possible that occupant mistook a cough in the street for that of an intruder. It was noted that the curtains in the room used as a study had not been drawn. It seems therefore possible that occupant mistook the lights of a passing car for those of an electric torch. The police car returned to headquarters at 02-35 hours.
>
> It may be worth noting that the occupant had called at the station an hour or so earlier, with a complaint about two men whose actions he had considered menacing. A written statement was taken and is attached.
>
> Mr. Compton appeared sober on both occasions.

When they had gone, I stood by the window gazing out into the night. The windows of the houses on the opposite side of the road were dark, and the street was deserted, and I knew that neither of those factors meant a thing. Somebody or something was there.

I wondered what would have happened if I had not dialled "999," if I had risked it and gone into the flat. I still wonder. I drew the curtains. Now all they had to watch was the front door. I was deadly tired, and went to bed, and fell asleep in a short while. But previous to going to bed I minutely examined my typewriter and typing paper and envelopes. I had set them in a special way.

They had not been disturbed. *That* was quite certain.

At four-thirty in the morning the telephone rang by my bed-side, and I thought I knew what to expect. But when I lifted the receiver nobody would speak to me.

After a while there was a click, and the dialling tone was renewed.

CHAPTER 6

The following morning I got up about eight-fifteen, as is my custom. I take about an hour and a half to have a bath, shave, dress, and eat a light breakfast. This is a long time, but during that period I read one morning paper in my bath, and another over breakfast. So that by about ten o'clock, I have, so to speak, cleared the deck, and absorbed as much of the day's news as I wish, and am ready for work.

I was trying to write an article for a Sunday newspaper, but found it impossible to concentrate. One of the things which worried me was whether to tell Juliet of the previous evening's incidents. In the end, I decided against it.

I felt that the crunch was still to come; that when it did I would need all the strength I could build up beforehand; that to tell all things to Juliet would involve keeping her courage up as well as my own. It was a cold-blooded assessment, and probably an incorrect one.

I met her for lunch for a drink and a smoked salmon sandwich. I thought she might feel a little embarrassed by the subject of her adoption, and that the best thing to do was to grab this whole subject by the throat at once. So immediately we met I gave a broad smile, and said:

"Fond as I am of your father and mother by adoption, I must admit that I never could imagine how they produced anybody as attractive as you, my darling, and I am absolutely delighted that they didn't!"

I have perhaps given the impression that in those days she was all mystery and brooding thoughtfulness. Such was far from the case. Most of the time she was extremely vivacious, and laughed easily and today she looked radiant after a long night's sleep. She appeared by now to think that my troubles were an amateurish and over-melodramatic attempt to prevent an investigation of Mrs. Dawson's life and death, simply because some members of her family or friends might be embarrassed.

"I expect the whole thing will die down in time. I mean, once they see you are not going to be intimidated, darling, they'll just stop all this nonsense," she said.

I forebore to tell her that Mrs. Dawson had no family to speak of, and few friends.

I recalled the men on the pavement, the flashing torch in my flat, the telephone call when nobody spoke, and said yes, yes, yes, I was sure she was right.

We only had a short meeting because she had a hair appointment at two o'clock. It was a happy meeting. I look back on it now and savour it, and remember it with tenderness.

In the afternoon I went to the London Library and took out some books on early Roman history, because I was still tampering with the idea of setting a crime in the Sibylline Caves, silly though it sounds. Then I had a hair-cut in Trumpers, and went home and found my evening paper thrust into the letter box, and there was Bunface, a single-column picture, in the middle of a front-page story.

She stared out of the page at me just as she had stared at me on the train from Brighton, when she wasn't dabbing at her eyes with the grubby handkerchief. The same round, uninteresting face, the same short cropped hair; all a little muzzy, all rather blurred, as snapshots are when they are enlarged beyond the capacity of the negative.

She had been strangled the previous evening in a narrow alley called Paradise Lane off Notting Hill Gate. Police were attempting to establish her identity. There were hints that she had been murdered by a mentally unbalanced person, though the headlines did not go so far as to invoke a "maniac killer."

I let myself in, and went straight over and mixed myself a whisky and soda, and thought, well, she knows now, she knows now all right, whether there is a life after death, and whether she will see her friend again. She had been toying with the idea of suicide, whether seriously or not one could not say, but that wasn't necessary, as it turned out, that wasn't necessary at all. Somebody else had done the job for her.

In these cases it is a delicate newspaper habit to talk about "good-time girls" rather than prostitutes, but even the newspapers, having seen her photograph, hadn't been able to justify the description of "good-time girl." She was described as "an unknown middle-aged woman." Police were anxious to talk to anybody who recognised her from the photograph. I wondered how the police had obtained the photograph, and assumed that they had found a snapshot in her handbag, perhaps a holiday snapshot of herself and her dead friend, and had enlarged it.

This then was the wretched, despairing old doll who had given me a letter containing veiled threats. This was the unhappy soul who had complained about me to the police. This was a woman who, I felt sure, was of such a weak and mediocre mentality that she had got caught up in machinations of which she knew little. Or did she? Either way, the result was the same for me, and now the result was the same for her. Knowing nothing of the stresses to which the jungle predators had subjected her, I cannot find it in my heart to say she should have stood firm.

Surprising as it may seem, it took me some minutes to appreciate how I was concerned. This is doubtless because a crime writer, though he may write of crimes, normally has had little personal involvement in such matters. In some ways he can be a proper little innocent.

When realisation dawned it came as a shock. This woman had laid a complaint against me, alleging that I had made improper suggestions to her in a train. Her photograph would indicate that such suggestions might have been very peculiar indeed, because she obviously had no pretensions at all to normal sex appeal. Her photograph would be recognised at the local police station, and her complaint on record.

She had been killed, it was hinted, by an unbalanced killer, not by a sex maniac, or by a berserk assassin lusting for blood, or by a robber, but by somebody who was peculiar in some unspecified way.

I was very anxious to get to the police station, before a police officer called on me. I kept telling myself that I was not nervous because I had nothing to be nervous about, but that it would look better if I came forward, as a volunteer with information, rather than if I sat back until I was approached.

I was waiting to cross Earls Court Road from Scarsdale Villas when a man's voice said, "Excuse me, sir." He only wanted to know the way to the Old Brompton Road. Yet the incident set my heart pounding, because I was so keen to report to the police station before the police called on me.

What exactly I was going to say about poor old Bunface, which I hadn't said already the previous day to Sergeant Matthews, I did not know.

In the event, I just walked in and up to the Enquiries counter. I had to wait a few minutes while a poorly dressed middle-aged woman gave her name and address and details of a purse which she had lost from her handbag. It was two minutes to six by the big white clock on the wall.

By five minutes past six she had finished describing in some detail the circumstances leading up to her loss. The station sergeant was a bright-looking, fair-haired man in his thirties. Her tale would make no difference. Either the purse would be found and handed in, or it wouldn't. But he listened patiently, sensing that in pouring out the details she was finding relief, even misguidedly believing that she was contributing something towards the recovery of her purse. He was doing a first-class public relations job. The police are very good at this sort of thing. It is an ancillary part of their work which is not sufficiently recognised, a psychotherapy for people in distress akin to that provided by the priest in the confessional.

As she turned away from the counter, he looked at me and said, "Yes, sir?" in the cheerful manner of a greengrocer dealing with the next customer in the queue. I watched the woman go out of the door, and heard the sergeant say, "Yes, sir?" again.

As he did so, another woman, younger, carrying a small dog, came through the door. I would rather have spoken to him on my own, but I could not delay any more. I said, as quietly as I could:

"There's a case in the papers about a murdered woman being found in Paradise Lane. I would like to have a word with somebody about her."

"I see, sir," he said, with as much interest as if I had been re-porting a stolen bicycle. He reached for a piece of paper.

"May I have your name, sir?"

"James Compton."

"Address?"

"274 Stratford Road—round the corner from here."

"I take it you have some information you wish to give, sir?"

"Yes, more or less."

"Could you give me some rough idea of the nature of the in-formation, sir? You'll understand that in cases of this kind we get a lot of—"

I misunderstood what he was going to say:

"Yes, I know, cranks and crackpots."

He smiled and said:

"Well, yes—but I was going to say a lot of duplicated informa-tion, not that we aren't glad to have it, of course, but it's just a question of who should see you, sir."

"Well, I travelled from Brighton with her in a train the evening before yesterday," I began. He interrupted me.

"Ah, now you're cooking with gas, sir!"

"I beg your pardon?"

"I mean that's interesting, sir. Just one minute—"

He made to move away from the counter. The woman with the dog had been pretending to read some police notices on the wall. She turned away from them and moved with studied casualness over to the counter. This was something she could not miss.

"Actually, Sergeant Matthews from this police station knows the story. I just thought if there were any other small details—you know? Well, I just thought I'd call in—in case, as it were."

"Sergeant Matthews knows the story?"

"He called yesterday morning."

"Yesterday morning, sir? The murder wasn't committed till the late evening, sir."

"He called about another aspect of the case—connected but different."

"Connected but different?"

"That's right."

The woman with the dog was stroking its head, pretending to be preoccupied with it, looking down at it. She was on my right side. I could almost see her left ear growing bigger. I wasn't going to say any more. Nothing about the pavement incident, or the lights in my flat, and the abortive search. She'd had enough free entertainment.

"Just a minute, sir," said the sergeant again, and disappeared into the back of the station.

After a few minutes he came back.

"Would you go into the waiting-room, sir? I'll show you where it is."

"I know where it is, I was there yesterday evening."

"I see, sir."

He gave me a thoughtful look, but he didn't ask why. He insisted on accompanying me to the waiting-room. I had a feeling he was afraid I might change my mind. As he shut the door behind me, I noticed that he could see the door from the Enquiries counter. I began to fill my pipe, and had hardly got the tobacco burning smoothly before a young plain-clothes detective came in.

He was tall and dark, with black curly hair and a fresh complexion. All bright and breezy and friendly, he was, and he slumped himself down on to a chair on the opposite side of the little table, and slapped a notebook and pencil down on to the table and said cheerily:

"Good evening, sir, you're Mr. Compton, I believe? What is it you want to tell us, sir?"

"I don't particularly wish to tell you anything. I just thought I'd call in and remind you that I met this murdered woman on a train from Brighton the evening before last. You know about it."

"We know about it?"

"Yes, they know about it here. She called later that evening and alleged I had made improper suggestions to her. Poor old thing," I added. "Poor old thing. I wouldn't think anybody had ever made suggestions to her improper or otherwise. Anyway, the station sergeant took note of her complaint, and your Sergeant Matthews called on me yesterday morning to tell me about it. I gathered that the desk sergeant here had already formed an opinion that she was—well, you know, a bit of a crackpot, but they felt they had to inform me officially and get a formal denial from me, and all that sort of thing."

"I see, sir."

He wasn't taking any notes at all.

"I mentioned one or two other things to Sergeant Matthews."

"What sort of things, sir?"

But I wasn't buying that one.

"Look," I said, "it's a long story. This woman gave me a message typed on my own typewriter and on my own typing paper. But it's all very complicated, and linked up with other things, and so I told all to Sergeant Matthews. I just called in here in case there was some other details you people wanted to know."

I watched him doodling with his cheap government pencil on a blank page of his notebook. After a while he said:

"Well, we appreciate that, sir, we appreciate that very much. Just for the record, perhaps you would give me a detailed description of the woman you travelled with from Brighton."

I described her without hesitation and without difficulty. When I had finished he said:

"Well, sir, the best thing I can do is to attach a note to the sergeant's report, saying you called, and if there's anything further we want, we'll get in touch with you. Right?"

"Fine," I said, and got to my feet. But he hesitated.

"Perhaps I'd better just look for the old sergeant's report, sir, as I haven't seen it. It's a big station here, we don't see everybody else's reports. I mean, that wouldn't be on the cards, would it? I mean, we can't see everybody's reports, can we? Otherwise we'd spend all our day reading. See what I mean? I mean, there might be some point or other we could clarify at once. So if you wouldn't mind just hanging on a minute, sir?"

I liked his eager, babbling incoherent manner. It was nice and friendly.

"It might save us troubling you further," he added, as an after-thought.

"Certainly, if you wish," I said, and sat down again. He went out of the room. He was a pleasant, ingenuous character, probably a young uniformed officer on probation to be a detective.

I waited for ten minutes. When the door opened again two other plain-clothes men came in. They were different.

One of them announced himself briefly as the superintendent in charge of what he called "the Paradise case." Later, he referred to the other man as "sergeant."

My first impression of the superintendent was of a tall, well-built man in his early fifties, with grey eyes, a good head of grey hair, dressed in a grey suit. His face seemed grey, too. It was a strong face, with a good brow and a firm but not cruel mouth. The nose was a little too long, and the chin was pointed rather than square, but it was a pleasant enough, intelligent face. He spoke good English with a strong voice, and had a slight north-country accent.

The sergeant, on the other hand, gave an impression of fawn-ness. He was shorter and stouter than the superintendent, and had a round, bullet head, a short nose, and a jaw and underlip which protruded aggressively. His hair was spread in bootlace style over a nearly bald skull, and was brown except for the grey bits above his ears. He had brown eyes, and wore a brown suit, and had a putty-coloured complexion. He was of about the same age as the superintendent but, I think, lacked the former's education and general intellect. He was more of the "old sweat" type of N.C.O. which one used to find in the Army.

They had, however, one dreadful thing in common—fatigue. It was not the superficial fatigue which can be shed by a good nine hours' sleep. It was something far deeper, something that had been built up over a long period of years. Just as the dirt and grime of certain industrial cities seems to become ingrained in the skins of the workers, so the greyness and the lines of fatigue were implanted on the faces of these two detectives. Their appearance spoke more forcefully than any leading article of a Force below establishment, of cancelled week-ends and shortened holidays, of long nights and days at work, and little appreciation, and no joy.

The superintendent held some typescript in his hand. He said:

"Good evening. You're Mr. James Compton, of 274 Stratford Road?"

"That's right. I just called in—"

"Yes, sir, thank you very much," he said quickly. "There are one or two points I want to clear up."

"Carry on," I said.

He gave me the impression of a man in a hurry, which is never very complimentary.

"Last night you were returning home, according to this station report, when you allege you were threatened by two men, at present unidentified. Right?"

"I thought only one man was actually threatening me. The other man—"

But he wouldn't let me finish.

"Well, anyway, you thought you were being threatened?"

"Correct," I said shortly.

"You reported the incident. Very properly. You then went to your flat in Stratford Road, where your suspicions were aroused, and you thought some person or persons unknown were in the flat. But a search showed your suspicions were apparently unfounded. Right?"

"Yes—you could put it that way."

The tired lines round his mouth deepened. He said:

"Look, sir, I don't want to put it any way except the correct way."

"Well, that's right," I said reluctantly. "But I think my suspicions were right, and I think it's connected with this woman in the train who complained about me."

He interrupted me again.

"Tell me about her, sir."

"There's not much to tell, and I've told Sergeant Matthews already."

He sat down opposite me. The sergeant shouted through the doorway, "Bert, bring another chair in, will you?" The superintendent waited until the sergeant was seated. Then he said:

"Tell me the story briefly, right from the beginning, sir."

"Going right back? Back to Mrs. Dawson and Pompeii?"

"Who's Mrs. Dawson?" he asked.

I guessed that Sergeant Matthews had not bothered to put in a report about anything other than the matter about which he had called.

I had a feeling he wouldn't do more than briefly mention what I had told him, because of the bored way he had put poor Bunface's communication in his notebook. But I hadn't expected him to put in no report at all.

There was nothing for it but to go over the whole thing again. I saw the bald-headed sergeant scribbling shorthand notes. When I had finished there was a silence.

The superintendent was picking at the wooden table with a pin he had found lying on it.

"Can you think of any reason why this unfortunate woman should have made any complaint against you, sir?"

"Certainly not, except that she was in a highly emotional state, and probably neurotic."

"Can you think of any reason why this woman, whom you had met for the first time, should know your name and address, unless you gave it to her for some purpose, and if you gave it to her, why did you?"

"I dealt with that point with Sergeant Matthews," I said. The

fawn-coloured sergeant spoke for the first time. He had a rasping
voice which contrasted with the superintendent's soft tones. He
sounded as though he had spent much of his life shouting at dogs,
or horses, or men.

"The superintendent here, he isn't Sergeant Matthews, sir. He
is just asking—"

"I know what the superintendent wants to know, and the answer is, I didn't give her my name and address and I don't know
how she got it."

I liked the grey superintendent, but I didn't like the fawn-
coloured sergeant with his jutting jaw and lower lip.

"About this message you think was written on your machine
and paper," began the sergeant.

"I don't think it was written on my machine. I *know* it was. So
does Sergeant Matthews, and so would you, if he'd written a proper
report. And if you'd read it, of course."

"Why should the message have been typed on your machine,
and taken down to the coast, and then brought up again, why
shouldn't it have just been put through your letter box or posted?"
asked the superintendent gently.

He had his left elbow on the table, his left hand supporting his
head, and was looking thoughtfully. I shook my head helplessly.

"I don't know," I said, "I just don't know. It doesn't make
sense."

"No, it doesn't," said the sergeant.

The superintendent made no comment.

Suddenly the whole thing infuriated me.

"Anyway, why should anyone wish to prevent me probing into
Mrs. Dawson's background? Why should they cook up all this
bloody nonsense?"

"There's a woman been killed," said the sergeant flatly. "You
come along here, and you say, yes, I travelled up with her in the
train, the evening before she was killed, and she must have been
very neurotic, you say, otherwise she wouldn't have made up some
story about me, you say. Right? And when we ask you a few simple
questions, what happens? You bang the table. You get all touchy.
Why?"

I didn't answer. When I spoke I looked at the superintendent, as if he had asked the questions.

"I am not getting touchy."

"I'm sure you're not," he said. "Sergeant, Mr. Compton is not getting touchy, why should he be touchy? He just misunderstood you."

He looked at me with his calm, tired eyes.

"Mr. Compton, I don't think you quite understand."

"No, I don't," I said, "I don't understand. I don't understand anything. I only know what I know, and that's what I've told Sergeant Matthews, and now you, and I called in here voluntarily to try to help you, and you go on at me. You go on at me so," I added indignantly.

"We're not going on at you," said the sergeant, in his rasping voice. "The superintendent here, he's just trying to clear up a few points. He's a busy man, you want to understand that. When a case like this happens, he's a busy man."

The superintendent said:

"I am going to ask you again a question I asked you earlier, but on a broader basis. I asked you whether you could think of any reason why this woman should have lodged a complaint against you—I now ask you whether you can think of any reason why you should *imagine* that this woman lodged a complaint against you?"

I stared at him, bewildered.

"Would you mind repeating that?"

"Can you think of any reason why you should imagine that this woman made an allegation against you, Mr. Compton?"

I sat back in my chair and looked at him again.

"Imagine it?"

He had turned half sideways to me and was filling his pipe from a grey rubber pouch.

"That, and other things."

"What things?"

"Can you think of any reason why two alleged thugs should try to intimidate you?"

"Only in connection with what I've told you."

"Can you think of any reason why a mysterious, unknown man should telephone you."

"Look," I said, "it's no good going on like that—you've got to accept the whole story in its entirety or not at all."

The sergeant had stopped writing shorthand. He was doodling idly. The superintendent had put a second match to his pipe. He said:

"The point is this, Mr. Compton. We cannot find any trace of a woman lodging a complaint against you at this station, or in fact at any station in the Metropolitan area."

The sergeant said:

"That's why the superintendent asked whether—"

He stopped speaking, but went on doodling, without looking up.

"Whether what, for God's sake?" I asked loudly.

"That's why I asked whether you thought she might have done—even if she didn't, sir," said the superintendent.

"Your records," I said quickly, "your records must be wrong. If you'll look through your records—"

"The other point is this," interrupted the superintendent, "we have no Sergeant Matthews at this station. And haven't had for years."

It was a pleasant evening outside, warm for October, the sky still blue, and I don't feel the cold physically as much as some; but in certain circumstances there is a mental chill, a kind of freezing up, which can be equally devastating. This I felt.

You know you are in a police station, and you know you have come there voluntarily; and you touch the chair you're sitting on, and the table in front of you, and you hear the traffic going past outside, and so you know you are alive; furthermore, you know you are not dreaming, because dreams move faster.

You can hear your heart beating, and feel a stickiness in the throat when you swallow, because if you are not dead, and not asleep and dreaming, there is only one reasonable conclusion at which you can arrive.

You fight against this conclusion; even those who really are mentally sick strenuously deny it, maintaining with a sad, forlorn

intenseness that it is they who are sane, the others who are mistaken.

I sometimes wonder if they hear the voices of others as from a
distance, echoing distortedly, as I did now.

"What is your job, sir?" asked the superintendent, with surprising gentleness.

"I write, I write books and articles. There's something wrong,"
I added urgently, "there's something wrong with the system, either
that or I am going mad. This Sergeant Matthews—"

"There is no police officer called Matthews who could have
called on you, sir," interrupted the bald-headed sergeant. "That's
what the superintendent has just said, loud and clear, sir. He said
there's no Sergeant Matthews attached to this station or any station
near here."

"Be that as it may," I began.

"Be that as it isn't," said the sergeant. "Facts are facts."

"Well, somebody calling himself Sergeant Matthews called," I
said angrily, "and I would like to say that I am not at all surprised,
upon reflection, that this woman made up a complaint. I am sorry
she has ended as she has, but she was in a highly emotional and
neurotic state."

Neither of them was looking at me.

"So I'm not surprised. Not at all surprised. Not really."

The superintendent got up and walked across the room, and
stared at the yellow painted wall. Without turning round, he said:

"I have tried to tell you that there is no record that this woman
made any complaint against you. Why do you insist that she did?"

"Because she did," I replied sullenly. "You've got it wrong
somewhere. Same as you have about Sergeant Matthews."

He came back and sat down again and said:

"You realise what you are saying, Mr. Compton?"

"Yes, I do."

"You are saying that you travelled with an unknown woman
who has now been killed?"

"Yes, I am—I'm saying that."

"You're saying that although you did not give her your name
and address, she somehow knew it?"

"Yes, I am."

"And laid a complaint against you?"

"And laid a complaint against me."

"And gave you a message you cannot now produce?"

"I can't produce it, because I handed it over to a police officer, at his request."

"You insist that she complained about you, although there is no record that she did?"

The sergeant was taking notes again. I felt an increasing need to be meticulously accurate.

"I insist," I said carefully, "that a police officer called on me and said she had made a complaint."

"And that the officer's name was Matthews?"

"And that he *said* his name was Matthews."

"And that somebody phoned you in the night?"

"Yes."

"Twice?"

"The second call might have been a wrong number."

"And that you were, in your view, menaced on a public footpath at night?"

"In my view, yes."

"And that on the self-same night a person or persons entered your flat, although a search revealed no signs of intruders?"

"Correct."

"You think you are being followed all the time?"

I shook my head. A feeling of helplessness came over me.

"Not all the time."

"Most of the time?"

"Probably most of the time. I don't know. How should I?"

"You feel your flat is under observation?" asked the sergeant.

"Yes."

"All the time?"

"How the hell do I know?"

"You think that all this elaborate business is just to frighten you out of investigating the background of another lady, this Mrs. Dawson?" asked the superintendent.

"This Mrs. Dawson, as you call her, yes, I do."

"Who was also murdered?"

"Who was also murdered," I muttered.

"His lady friends seem kind of accident prone," murmured the sergeant, looking up, looking at the superintendent, not looking at me. The superintendent said:

"Can you suggest any other reason why all this rigmarole should be organised against you?"

I banged the table with the palms of both my hands and stood up, looking down at the superintendent and the sergeant.

"Look, I have had enough of this!" I said, and almost shouted the words. "I've just about bloody well had enough of this!"

"I expect you have," said the superintendent, and nodded.

"Too bloody true, you have," said the sergeant.

"I'm an ordinary citizen, leading an ordinary life, and I'm being persecuted, and when I seek the assistance of the police, what bloody well happens?"

"Imaginary policemen call on you with imaginary complaints, voices ring you up in the early hours, that's what happens," said the sergeant abruptly, tapping his protruding lower lip with his Stationery Office Pencil.

"You mustn't take too much notice of the old sergeant, here, he's a down-to-earth character," murmured the superintendent.

He looked at the sergeant expressionlessly, neither approvingly nor disapprovingly. He looked as though he had heard it all before, not once, but many times.

"Women in trains give him messages typed on his own type-writer, and footpads menace him," muttered the sergeant. "And thieves break into his flat and steal nothing, and quietly make off. What a life!"

The superintendent took no notice. He said:

"Have you been victimised much in your life, Mr. Compton? Had much bad luck, one way and another? Made a lot of enemies, through no fault of your own? That sort of thing?"

I shook my head and gathered my packet of cigarettes and lighter from the table and put them in my pocket. There was nothing more I could say.

I was feeling the heat from the electric lighting, and the voices of the superintendent and sergeant were not so clear, and the noises of the traffic outside had grown dimmer. I had a feeling of panic, an impression that I was indeed losing my grip on reality.

"I can describe him," I heard myself say.

"Describe who?" said the sergeant. "The unknown voice who rang you up?"

"He was a middle-aged sergeant," I went on doggedly, "with a fresh complexion, and a bald head, and he was rather stout, and he had brown eyes."

They were looking at me placidly, as people look at a child reciting a poem. But I forced myself to go on.

"He came on a bicycle, and wore bicycle clips on his trousers. And he said his name was Matthews, Sergeant Matthews, of Kensington Police Station. You say he doesn't exist and couldn't have brought a complaint. Can't you suggest something? Can't you help me? What am I to think?"

I rubbed my forehead with the fingers of my right hand, and looked down to where the superintendent was still sitting at the table, and saw him watching me with more attention.

"Why did you go to Italy, where this Mrs. Dawson was killed?" he asked quietly.

"I'd had a car accident and was a bit run down. My legs had been slashed a bit," I said indifferently, and moved to the door.

"They say car accidents can make you sleep badly," he said, getting to his feet.

"Yes, I was sleeping badly. I'm all right now, though."

"I'm sure you are."

"Nasty shock, a bad car accident," said the sergeant mildly.

The superintendent asked:

"Did you sleep well in Italy?"

"After the first few days."

"Chap I knew was in a car accident," said the sergeant. "Went round for some time afterwards thinking he'd got a radio set in his head. All right now, though. Still, it just shows."

I paused and stared at him.

"That's usually a sign of schizophrenia. That's not delayed shock. That's got nothing to do with car accidents," I said quickly.

"Hasn't it, sir? Well, maybe he was schizo anyway. Better now. They cure all sorts of things these days."

He had dropped his hectoring tone. He got to his feet, and took a packet of cigarettes from his pocket and offered me one.

The three of us stood near the closed door of the waiting-room. Almost like three acquaintances who had satisfactorily concluded a difficult business deal, except that my stomach muscles were still contracted and I wanted desperately to get out of the place. But the superintendent was leaning against the door, and the sergeant was near him, and I was on the inside of the room.

"Well, I must go now," I said firmly, and walked towards them, but they didn't move. I had to stop. The grey superintendent glanced casually at me, and then back to the sergeant. They began talking between themselves, as if I wasn't there.

The superintendent said, yes, of course, it was a question of early diagnosis, and early treatment, like everything else in medical matters. The sergeant said, "well, yes, sir, but that was the whole difficulty, getting people to have treatment, especially in certain cases.

"You can't get 'em certified," he said in a low voice, "unless they're right round the bend, I mean, so long as they can look after themselves, more or less—and probably less than more—and so long as they're not causing what you might call a public nuisance, you can't do anything about it. And that's the trouble."

The superintendent said:

"And more's the pity, both for their sakes and everybody's."

"They've got to go voluntary," said the sergeant.

"Doctors are reluctant to certify," said the superintendent, "and it's not surprising—one mistake, and bingo, they're sued for damages. It's a pity, really."

"It is, sir."

"A bit of treatment, and they're free of it all. No more radio sets in their heads, no more voices out of the ether, no more feeling that the whole world's against them, spying on them, and all that lark. They're happy."

"But they won't go, sir. They won't go, not voluntarily," said the sergeant regretfully.

I felt that if I didn't leave at once that very instant, the pressure building up inside me would burst, and I would jump at the door, and push them aside, and run out, though I knew I wouldn't get far.

They were too cautious, too experienced, to say what they meant openly to me. They accepted that I had been in the same train as sad Bunface. They had to, because I had described her so minutely.

But they didn't accept anything else.

They thought I heard voices, and dreamed dreams, and saw visions. One had the impression that in a long career of interviewing all sorts and kinds of people, they had formed mental patterns of how people behaved in certain circumstances, and what could happen and what could not.

"It's been a waste of time," I said bitterly. "Your time and mine. You can't cope, and I suppose I don't blame you, because you're faced with a situation you've never experienced before."

"Oh, yes, we have," said the sergeant defensively.

"There's just one last question, sir," said the superintendent, making no move from the door.

I was wondering when they would ask it.

"Go on," I said, "I can guess it."

"It's just a formality, Mr. Compton, nothing for you to worry about. More a question of tidying up loose ends, if you know what I mean, seeing that you've come forward and admitted to an encounter with this Paradise Lane woman, which we didn't know about—and seeing that you got the idea she laid a complaint against you. If we can just clear it up now, then there won't be anything more to worry about."

"No, nothing more to worry about," I muttered.

"Where were you between say eleven-thirty last night, and one-thirty this morning, sir? That's putting it a bit baldly, of course, but it's just for the record. You're an intelligent man, and—"

"Am I," I interrupted sharply. "Am I indeed? Just now you were saying I needed mental treatment."

I saw them both stiffen, suddenly look less relaxed, more alert. When the sergeant spoke he could have been addressing a child of ten. He didn't exactly pat me on the head, but his tone was patient and coaxing.

It nearly made me sick.

"Now, now, now, sir, the superintendent wasn't saying any such thing, were you, sir? Nor was I."

"We were just making a few general remarks, Mr. Compton. I don't think you have any call to suggest we meant them personally."

"No call at all," said the sergeant.

I turned away from them and walked to the opposite side of the room. As I did so, I heard the superintendent say:

"I have to inform you, Mr. Compton, that if you would rather say nothing, and await the arrival of a legal adviser, that is your right."

I swung round and looked at them, the tall, grey one, and the shorter fawn one, so different in appearance, so different in manner: one apparently kindly, one mostly harsh and rasping. A good orchestration. Lifting you up and slapping you down. But both tired and over-worked. I think it explained a good deal.

I shook my head.

"I know all that. I don't need a legal adviser to recall to me what I was doing for a couple of hours last night."

"Well, let's have it then," said the sergeant with surprising directness. "Let's have the times and places, then we can pack it up for the moment."

He went over to the table by the window, sat down briskly, and flipped open his notebook.

"At eleven-thirty, I was still talking to my future father-in-law."

"Okay," he said. "At eleven-thirty you were still with him."

"At eleven-forty-five, I left him and walked down Kensington Church Street. At around midnight, or a bit before I was here."

"Here?"

"Yes, here waiting around, making out a statement for some plain-clothes police officer. It took about an hour. Just before one o'clock I was with your officers at my house."

"Not our officers. Kensington officers. We're Scotland Yard."

"Well, police officers."

"Finding nothing and nobody?"

"Finding nothing and nobody."

"And after that?" asked the superintendent, in his quiet voice. "After that, what?"

"After about one-thirty, nothing. I was in bed. But that covers the period, that covers me till one-thirty in the morning."

"That's right," said the sergeant, looking up from his book. "That covers you till one-thirty in the morning, that's okay, sir. That covers the gentleman till one-thirty in the morning," repeated the sergeant, looking at the superintendent.

I should have let well alone, but I can never resist a crack. It's probably the Irish streak in my blood, not the Dutch or the English.

"So you can go and see them and check up," I said coldly. "Apart from a few minutes walking down Church Street when I was observed by two men you don't think exist, you can go and see them. Ask them more questions, check the times again, get more signed statements, do what you damned well like."

"We'll do that thing," said the sergeant, cheerfully. "We'll do just that thing, sir."

But I still couldn't let well alone, because I was still resentful of their implications.

"Unless you think the plain-clothes officer in this station who took my statement was a figment of my imagination? Unless you think the uniformed officers who searched my flat at my request are non-existent?" I said sarcastically. "And the patrol car was a sort of ghost car? I'm going now," I added. "I came here with good-will, but I would have done better to stay away."

The sergeant got up hurriedly from his chair, and moved to the door. His purpose might have been to open the door for me, but I knew it wasn't. If anything, his object was to keep it closed.

"And at three o'clock this morning?" asked the superintendent quickly. "Say between one-thirty and three o'clock?"

"What's three o'clock got to do with it, superintendent?"

"That's about when she died—give a bit, take a bit, sir."

"He's been edging up to it, so as not to tax your memory too much at one and the same time," said the sergeant.

CHAPTER 8

Y ou're all right between eleven-thirty and one-thirty, now what about one-thirty to three o'clock? What about then?"

"I was in bed, in bed and probably asleep."

"Anybody else in the flat, Mr. Compton?"

"No."

"Anybody to support that statement?" asked the sergeant.

"Probably."

"Name? And address, if you know it?"

I shook my head, and began to walk towards them, towards the door. I had come of my own accord, I could go of my own accord, unless they were going to arrest me on the spot and prefer a charge. I knew it, and they knew it. More important, they knew that I knew it.

"I don't know the names and addresses. The witnesses I mean are the people who have got me under observation. Me and the flat. Day and night."

"Oh, that lot," said the sergeant.

The superintendent said gently:

"The ones who are persecuting you? The people whose voices you hear on the telephone, who type messages to you on your own typewriter, and try to attack you in the street?"

I nodded. I found myself unable to say more, and walked out without being obstructed in any way.

I think they were glad to be rid of me. At any rate for the moment.

Outside the light was failing now. I stood on the steps of the police station, breathing deeply, watching the traffic move slowly past, thinking about the man calling himself Sergeant Matthews, trying to discern somewhere some clue, and finding no answer.

I walked to the edge of the pavement, waiting for a gap in the traffic. Suddenly I saw what I thought might be an opportunity to nip across the road. A blue car was following a bus, with some distance in between. I believed I could make it, and took a step into the roadway, but the car was travelling faster than I had at first realised, and I stepped back and waited, and between the narrowing distance as the car closed up to the bus, I happened to glance at the corner of a side road some way up Earls Court Road.

It seemed to me that the men standing at the corner were looking in my direction. One was tall and wore drain-pipe trousers, and a short, dark, knee-length mackintosh-type coat. The other was of medium height and stockily built.

Then the traffic closed in. When it thinned again the corner was deserted except for a woman passing with a child.

I looked back at the police station, but I knew it was out of the question, I couldn't go back in there and say I thought I had just seen the two men who had menaced me on my way back from Juliet's home. I hesitated, but for no more than a few seconds.

I couldn't do it. I couldn't face them again.

I consoled myself with the thought that I was probably mistaken, and that it was two other men, but I knew it was lack of moral courage.

I could imagine the sergeant now saying, "Proper old persecution complex that one has, sir. Proper ripe one, that one is. Well, we get 'em all, don't we, sir? We get 'em all, the short and the tall, and a few nuts thrown in for good measure."

There was no question of going back.

All right, so the tired and over-worked superintendent and sergeant took a rugged, conventional view of me. Maybe they weren't as tactful as they might have been.

But now I knew, in effect, what it was like to have no police force to which one could appeal.

Now I knew what it was like to have the jungle about you, as you walked along the dangerous paths, and you were on your own, and there were eyes upon you, and there was no police force to which you could run for protection.

I appreciate these things now, but at the time I nurtured harsh feelings.

I went back to the flat and washed, and the evening paper with poor Bunface's picture on the front page was where I had left it, and I picked it up, and when I left the flat to call for Juliet I double mortice–locked the door.

In addition to the Yale-type lock I had a double mortice affair, though I had never used it. You turn the key twice in the mortice lock, and by and large it is burglar proof, short of cutting out the lock or battering down the door.

We went to Soho, to an Italian restaurant for dinner. One of the things which had surprised me was the calm way Juliet had accepted the news of the complaint laid against me by poor Bunface. I did not understand one of the simplest facts of life. If a woman loves you, then you are in the right if it is a question of simple, straightforward matters, and anybody who complains about you is a liar. There is no argument about it.

Juliet made no reference to anything of significance as we drove to Soho. This surprised and pleased me.

When we were seated in the restaurant I said: "Have you seen the evening papers? There was a murder quite near you."

She nodded equably.

That's one of the things about modern life. Murder means nothing, unless it affects you personally. In Anglo-Saxon times, when peasants were thin on the ground, murder was a serious matter. It was the loss of a pair of hands to the community. The hue and cry was raised, and everybody by law had to drop what they were doing and bring the criminal to book. Things are different now, because there are so many of us. We can afford losses.

"Seen her picture?" I asked.

She was looking at the menu, preoccupied. She nodded. I said:

"That was the woman on the train from Burlington and Brighton."

She put the menu down and took off her dark framed spectacles, and stared across the table at me, her face magnolia-pale in the lamp light.

"Are you sure?"

"Certainly I am."

"You must go to the police, darling."

"I've been."

"What did they say?"

"Various things. They said she had never made a complaint against me, for one thing."

"But what about the—?"

"What are you having as a first course?"

A waiter was standing by her shoulder. We chose our food and the waiter moved away.

"They said the man who called on me wasn't a police officer," I went on. "They hardly believed a word I said, except that I had been in the train with her."

She stared down at the table cloth, picking at a roll of bread with her left hand.

"Didn't you ask them for help or advice, or something?"

"More or less, yes."

"Well, I mean, what did they *say*? They can't have just said, 'we don't believe you,' they must have said *something*, put forward some theory. I mean, this is serious!"

I shrugged and ordered a carafe of red wine from the wine waiter.

"They kind of skated around things."

"They can't skate round them, darling."

"Well, they did."

"Didn't you press them for heaven's sake?"

"What for, sweetheart?"

"Well—investigations. And protection."

"Investigations of what? Protection against what? A message typed on my own typewriter which I can't produce? A 'phone call from an unknown man? Thugs who didn't attack me? People who come into my flat and aren't seen? Old ladies who won't co-operate? Men who hire policemen's uniforms—if he did hire it?"

She didn't answer, and did not have to, because the spaghetti bolognese arrived. She bent over it, but after a few seconds she gave me one of her quick, silent, secretive looks.

"Don't go and get all withdrawn," I protested. "You don't understand."

"No, I don't understand. Something ought to be done. You ought to have demanded it."

"Look, to the police a crime has two motives—a money motive in one form or another, or a sex motive of some sort. They asked, in effect, if I could supply a motive for them to work on. And I can't. If money or sex comes into it, it's so well hidden that I can't begin to see it."

She bent down and picked up the evening paper which I had placed on the floor by the table, and looked at the picture.

"There might be a sex angle, from what you told me," she murmured. "I suppose it's possible."

I hesitated, thinking over what she had said.

"There might be," I conceded reluctantly. "I suppose there just might be, in a twisted sort of way. But I doubt it."

"So do I," said Juliet.

"Individual jealousy perhaps? A coincidence."

Juliet nodded. I said:

"You should have seen her, darling, all overwrought and preoccupied with her own sad world. I think she almost forgot why she had been told to travel with me, I think at the end she almost forgot to give me the envelope. I think they had some sort of hold on her at one time, but now—"

I paused, trying to work it out, trying to think it through.

"Now she was almost free," said Juliet in such a low voice that I could hardly catch the words.

"Her tragedy, her grief and her sorrow, which seemed to her pointless—had liberated her."

In that cheap Italian restaurant I had caught a faint gleam of something valuable. Juliet had caught it, too, and was looking at me with shining eyes.

The waiter arrived with the next course.

You can't go on thinking about the Infinite with a grilled sole and chips in front of you. The moment passed. But I often recall it with a whiff of the old excitement. It has been a solace to me at times.

"That's why they killed her," said Juliet.

"Because she was free, or overwrought, or both, and couldn't be trusted."

"And might talk," added Juliet. "And might talk particularly to you."

She had put on her glasses to eat her fish, and the dark frames contrasted with her pale skin.

"About what, for God's sake?"

Juliet shook her head. We were back to square one. We ate in silence.

"That's why they may kill *you,* if you go on, darling, they're afraid of what you might discover," she said at last.

I guessed she had been using the seconds to gather her self-control. She gave me one of her fleeting glances over the top of her spectacles, and then looked down again.

"Oh, rot!" I said, and laughed. "This is a civilised country."

"That's what *she* thought. Maybe Mrs. Dawson thought Italy was a civilised country, too. Both strangled. A sort of roving executioner?"

She had pushed aside her food, and put down her knife and fork. I saw her upper lip trembling. I said:

"Look, if they'd wanted to do me in, they could have done so two or three times already."

She shook her head violently.

"I'm sure they don't *want* to kill you! Why should they?—you're so silly sometimes. Killing people is dangerous."

"Well, then, there you are!"

"But they will in the end—in the end they will, if they can't frighten you enough."

"Do you want me to be frightened enough? Is that what you really want?"

"I don't want it. But I could love you just as much, darling. You understand that? I want us to be happy and—unfrightened, and undead. I just want you to pretend to be frightened."

"And give in," I said. "Is that it?"

"And give in," she said. "If you've got the courage to."

"I don't think it's fair to put it that way."

"I don't suppose you do."

We stared across the table at each other, defiantly, each a little hurt.

"I'll think it over," I said at length.

I could feel bits and pieces of emotion churning around inside me, Irish combativeness, Boer obstinacy and tenacity, and the cool Anglo-Saxon tendency to compromise. To be of mixed blood is a mixed blessing.

"I'll think it over," I said again.

"That means you'll just go on as before."

She looked helplessly round the restaurant, adjusting her glasses, as if somewhere she might find aid and inspiration.

"It's silly," she murmured. "The world is full of ideas and things to write about. I think you've become obsessed with this idea."

"That's not the point."

"What is the point?"

"I just don't like—being pushed around, that's all."

"That's what I mean. Obstinacy, or pride, or something men seem to specialise in—it's made you obsessed."

"I said I would think it over. Anyway, I can't do anything at the moment. It's all one way. I can't telephone anyone, I can't write anywhere. I've got no contact."

"You will have—they'll try and bend you, and if you won't bend, they'll just lose patience, they'll just—"

She didn't finish the sentence. I asked her if she wanted fruit or coffee, because one had to say something.

She got abruptly to her feet. She said she was tired, and that she wanted to go home, and on the way out of the restaurant I heard her say something to the effect that one couldn't tell when the last chance would come, one couldn't tell at which precise point they would decide to finish the whole business off.

We drove sadly towards her home, most of the way in silence.

"It's probably all bluff," I said, at one point, ill-advisedly.

"Two other people thought that," she snapped.

"Might have been coincidence," I muttered.

"Oh, my God, oh, dear God, don't let's go over it again, darling! You didn't tell me what the police said."

I pulled the car up outside her house.

"I couldn't produce any evidence."

"So what?"

"I think they thought I was suffering from a persecution complex or something. They kept talking about radio sets in people's heads, and all that nonsense. The trouble was, I mentioned the car accident. That's what set them off. After-effects of shock, and stuff like that. That's why I got nowhere, really. Not that I'd have probably got anywhere anyway. They weren't Kensington officers, they were Scotland Yard types," I added.

"What difference does that make?"

"Not much, I suppose."

"Well, why did you mention it?"

"I just did, I mentioned it in passing, that's all. I just said they were from Scotland Yard, not the local station. What's wrong with that?"

"Nothing's wrong with that."

We sat in the car, staring straight ahead, aloof once again.

"You can see their point of view," Juliet said quietly.

"You mean *you* can see their point of view."

"Scotland Yard have got experience, darling, in all sorts of things."

"Of course they have."

Suddenly she turned to me and put her arms round my neck

and kissed me. I felt the pent-up annoyance which had been in her melting away, and her lips, which had been cold and dry, became slowly warm and moist.

"I do love you," she said. "And I'm sure everything is going to be all right. And don't worry, my sweetheart. Above all, don't worry. We'll soon be married, and on our own, and I will look after you—so don't do any more worrying. Promise?"

I nodded in the darkness of the car.

"Don't worry about the woman in the train, or messages written on your typewriter, or telephone calls in the night—or anything. Try to forget them. Promise?"

I disengaged myself gently, and felt suddenly chilled and lonely.

Outside the car, the night sky was dark. It had clouded over suddenly. A few spots of rain were appearing on the windscreen. I licked my lips and said:

"Look, a few moments ago, it was you who was worrying."

"I know, darling. I was silly. I'm better now."

"Why?" I asked abruptly. "Why are you better? You can't be worried sick one moment, and not the next—not without some reason."

"I just think it will all peter out. After all, this is a civilised country, like you said, Jamie."

"And the Lucy Dawson story?" I said as casually as I could. "What about the Lucy Dawson story?"

She didn't answer for a few seconds. They were the sort of seconds which make a mockery of man-made methods of recording time. I stared out of the car window into the blackness of some gardens, waiting for the answer I dreaded. A gust of wind blew a wet leaf against the car window, splat, and I jerked my head back, thinking it was a moth. I hate moths.

In the end, she gave the answer I feared.

"I should go ahead with it, darling. But don't work too hard. Promise?"

"I promise I won't work too hard."

I repeated her words automatically, staring at the wet leaf on the window.

"Why not chuck it for a bit, my love—come back to it with a fresh mind? Perhaps after our wedding, and after another holiday in the sun?"

"I have already told you I don't know how to get in touch with them."

I had spoken the words before I realised the futility of them, in view of what I knew she was thinking.

"They'll get to know somehow," she answered uneasily.

I turned the ignition key, preparatory to starting the engine.

"I know what you're trying to tell me, Juliet."

Across the road the door of her house suddenly opened. I saw in the light above the door the figure of old snuffly Stanley and two other men. One was the grey superintendent, and the other, shorter, I guessed to be the sergeant, though his back was turned to me.

"There they are," I said. "There they are, the Scotland Yard types, who've got so much experience about so many things. Tidying up the loose ends, so to speak."

I leant across her and opened the car door for her.

"Good night, darling. I should go and have a word with them. Compare notes about people who have nervous breakdowns, and think they're being persecuted. You'll have a lot to talk about, won't you?"

I heard her sob as she got out of the car, without a backward glance. They were bitter and cruel words, and I regret them now.

CHAPTER 9

I returned to my flat, and went to sleep at about one-thirty in the morning, or possibly a little later.

Until that time I sat in an easy chair, the curtains drawn, looking at the empty grate, and finally lay in bed staring into the darkness.

Once, before I went to bed, I walked to the windows and drew the curtains aside and gazed down into the deserted street. Opposite, the dark windows of the houses stared back, disinterested, negative and lifeless.

I guessed that I had hardly moved from the windows before somebody was writing in a notebook: *At ten minutes past midnight subject came to the windows and looked out. At twenty minutes past midnight subject switched off the lights in the living-room, and appeared to have retired for the night.*

Did he then, having scribbled his little notes, take a few minutes off, scuttle to a gas-ring and brew himself a cup of tea or instant coffee, before settling down to another long vigil? Or did some mate, fellow worker, joint-operator, or whatever he called himself, take over? Did they work four-hour shifts, or two-hour shifts, or what?

At one stage, I was tempted to leave the flat and go for a walk. What would happen? Would somebody attempt to follow me, unnoticed in the deserted streets? And if I challenged him what innocent story would he produce?

I guessed they would make no such attempt. They must know I would do nothing worth observing at that time of night. It was they, not I, who had need of concealment in the hours of darkness.

It was not the peasant who had need to lurk in the undergrowth.

Nevertheless, at one point I was tempted to put the matter to the test. It was after a moment of panic after I had gone to bed and put the lights out.

While I had the light on, I was sure of myself and of my facts, as I had been most of the time up to the present. But in the darkness one feels alone and unsure.

It was Juliet's *volte-face* which made me now feel hot and frightened. I was not afraid of attempted assassination. It was the need to know if my mind was in all truth working normally.

In a situation of apparent unreality and confusion, you need one person to lean on, one person to say, "Other people are wrong, but I know that what you say is the truth; not merely the truth as it appears to you, but the real truth. These things have happened, and you have not imagined them. You are not suffering from nerve troubles, you are mentally sound."

I had been, first, hurt and resentful, and then, as one does with those you love, I had begun to rationalise in her favour. I told myself that she was eager to take the police point of view, because although it conjured up temporary difficulties, at least it meant that my life was not in danger. She had jumped at the lesser of the two evils, and though, like the police, she had not patted me on the head, she had, in effect, said, "There, there, just take it easy, and when we are married mummy will look after you, and nobody's going to hurt you."

In the light, it was a consolation; in the darkness, with the blackness pressing in, and now and then the sound of rain beating against the windows, I realised how alone I now was in this matter.

"You are one," he had said on the 'phone, and he had proved his point. I could almost hear him, distantly, in the darkness, laugh like a green woodpecker, high, undulating, and mocking. And now, in a half-asleep condition, I began to wish for strange things to happen so that I could triumphantly come into physical touch with reality.

I imagined "Sergeant Matthews" calling again, on some pretext, and myself, ludicrously, tearing off a uniform button and retaining it as proof of his existence; or the same man handing back the message Bunface had given me, saying I could keep it as a souvenir; and there it would be, a proof for me, if for nobody else, that I had not been imagining things; indeed, I wished at one moment that even the telephone might ring in the darkness.

The telephone remained silent, but a board creaked somewhere. My first instinct was to reach for the bedside lamp, yet I hesitated.

If my mind was normal, and it was a man, then for better or for worse I could cope with him and be glad to do so. But if such were not the case, then what would I see? What heraldic animal, what figure from the past, what spirit from another world?

I lay for a few seconds, sweating, struggling back to full consciousness, before I pressed the light switch and saw that the room was empty.

It was at this moment that I was tempted to dress again, and go out into the wet streets, in the strange hope that after some minutes, glancing back, I would see a figure following at a distance.

I gave up the idea, because the experiment would prove nothing. If I could imagine other things, I could imagine that I was being followed; and if, lurking around a corner, I suddenly retraced my steps and tackled the man, he would deny that he was following me. It would be his word against mine. What was mine worth?

Nevertheless, one thing now was clear: if I could reason as logically as that, there was nothing wrong with my mind. The reasoning might have been faulty, but it satisfied me.

I switched off the light, and went to sleep without difficulty.

All that night I was left in peace.

It was almost as if, having inserted the yeast, they were leaving it to ferment the mixture. And in the morning, as I was having my breakfast, I saw an item in the newspaper which finally obliterated all doubts about my mental condition. It was a letter tucked away at the foot of the correspondence column and read:

> THE PRISONERS' FRIEND
> Sir,
>
> I have been awaiting the publication of some tribute to Mrs. Harold Dawson, Lucy Dawson to her friends, whose seemingly pointless murder at Pompeii must have shocked so many of her friends. As a Governor of one of H.M. prisons for many years, I came into contact with the wonderful work she carried out, unobtrusively, and indeed secretly, for the rehabilitation of released prisoners.
>
> Hers was largely an individual effort, without the backing of any of the devoted organisations which now carry out this work. She had no office and she had no staff, yet there must be many former criminals who today owe their present happiness and honest prosperity to her tireless work on their behalf.
>
> Let their gratitude be her memorial.
> A. Pearson Lt. Col. (Ret.)
> 14 BENTON HOUSE,
> LONDON, S.W.1.

I read the letter through twice with rising excitement.
Here, somewhere, might lie an obscure motive for her murder.

I finished my breakfast quickly, grabbed a notebook, and took a taxi to Benton House, which lay behind Eaton Square. On the way, my mind revolved round theories of the psychological reaction of some people towards other people who have helped them including the old one about the desire to strike down the benevolent Father Figure, though in Lucy Dawson's case it would be the Mother Figure.

I wondered whether Scotland Yard would note the letter, and send a copy to the Italian police, and interview the colonel. Perhaps the colonel could supply a list of names of people she had assisted in the past. Perhaps, somewhere on the list would be the name of one who was again in trouble, who had attempted to extort further assistance, or, if not assistance, then money.

I remembered the pencil marking on her map of Pompeii, and how her meeting with the killer must have been a planned one.

I had a feeling, as I read the letter, that if my well-being was in danger—and I was only on the fringe, so far—then what about the colonel's? Perhaps that was why I was in such a hurry to see him.

I do not know about subconscious instincts, but I know that by the time my taxi had reached Sloane Street I was aware of a feeling of desperate urgency.

Somebody felt himself menaced by Mrs. Dawson's past activities. Somebody with power, riches and organisational ability. Somebody who, as Juliet had pointed out during her period of anxiety, was sufficiently cautious to prefer to gain his means by fear rather than risk a killing, if this could be avoided. But somebody who would kill, if need be; who might consider, if he had read the letter, that there was no time to try psychological warfare as far as Colonel Pearson was concerned.

Benton House was a block of old-fashioned mansions turned into flats. I do not think I would have been surprised to find a couple of police cars and an ambulance outside, and a crowd of people being kept back by a constable, and although I saw that the little road was clear, I was still in doubt about what I would find when I reached his flat.

I glanced at the board showing the tenants' names and saw that his flat was on the second floor. There was an old-fashioned lift, but the cage was in use somewhere at the top of the building, so I ran up the two flights of stairs, and rang the bell.

I was just in time, but not in the way I had imagined.

A small, dapper man in check tweeds, well-polished shoes, and wearing a regimental tie opened the door. He was thin, aged about seventy, with a good head of white hair clipped close round the ears, bright blue eyes and a weather-beaten face.

"Colonel Pearson?"

"Come in—they're in the kitchen. Just give 'em a rub up," he said.

I hesitated.

"What are in the kitchen?"

"Aren't you Brigadier Robertson's son?"

When I shook my head he smiled and said:

"Sorry—sold my guns to the Brigadier last week. He didn't want to take 'em then. Said his son would pick 'em up this morning. I was getting worried. Just off in an hour or so."

He beckoned me in and pointed to some piled luggage in the hall. There were two old-fashioned cabin trunks, a black tin trunk with his name and regiment painted on it in white, an old, battered suitcase, held together with a strap, two fishing rods, binoculars, an ash walking-stick, a mackintosh, and an overcoat. I said:

"Going away for a bit? You're lucky, with the winter coming on."

"Going away for good. Going to live in Portugal," he said shortly. "Can't afford to live in England. Been struggling to keep this flat going for the last ten years since my wife died. Can't afford it, or anything else, as far as I can see."

He looked at me with angry blue eyes.

"Serve your country—thirty years in the Army, and fifteen in the Prison Service, and your country sees to it you can't afford to live in it. Bad show, you know, dam' bad show. Still, there you are! What can I do for you?"

"I saw your letter in the paper this morning," I said, and told what I had in mind. He nodded.

"Poor old Lucy Dawson—bad show. Don't understand it, I don't understand it. Come into the drawing room."

I followed him in, and he stood in front of the empty fireplace, looking around him forlornly.

"Bit of a mess in here. Sold the contents of the flat, lock, stock, and barrel. Sorry to go, but there you are. Still a British colony in Portugal, I'm told. Hope to make a few friends in time. Miss the Hampshire trout—still, can't be helped. Given up shooting anyway. Like to see 'em alive, rather than dead. Don't mind eating 'em, though."

He began to fill a Lovat Fraser–type pipe from an old-fashioned, black leather tobacco pouch.

"About Mrs. Dawson," I said.

"Lucy Dawson—it's simple enough. Got in touch with me when I was Governor of Parkway Prison, up in the Midlands. Asked me to keep an eye open for intelligent young first offenders who might do all right when they came out—given a chance. Not many, just ones I felt sure about—as far as you can ever feel sure of that type. Said she couldn't handle many. Maybe one or two a year, not more. Think she was in touch with one or two other Governors, also with a women's prison."

He paused to put a match to his pipe, and sucked in and blew out big clouds of smoke, tamping the glowing tobacco down with his forefinger as though his finger was heat proof.

"How did she find them jobs, Colonel Pearson? Can you tell me?"

"That was the trouble. Always is. Especially with these types. She wanted special types who might really make their way in the world, given a chance. Field was limited. Couldn't ask banks to take 'em on, could you? Nothing like that, if you see what I mean. But she succeeded all right. Wonderful woman."

He shook his head admiringly.

"She just went around, you know—interviewing people who might help. Heads of firms. People like that. Nobody knew, except the Governor of the prison, and the head of the firm. She depended upon me, or whatever Governor she was dealing with. It was a tricky do, I can tell you. But it worked."

"No failures?" I asked.

"None, as far as I know. And she kept in touch, you know.

With them and with me. Had a card from her shortly before the tragedy. Sent a wreath, as a matter of fact, for old times' sake."

"You sent a wreath?" I repeated. "There was only one wreath."

He took his pipe out of his mouth and stared at me in astonishment.

"Only one wreath? None from all those others?"

I shook my head.

"But that's awful!"

The disillusion on his face touched me.

"People forget," I said uneasily. "Time passes. People forget."

"That lot wouldn't forget. I told you, she kept in touch with them."

"Perhaps they didn't read about it—or didn't know where to send a wreath."

He clutched at the last possibility.

"That's probably it—they didn't know where to send a wreath. Otherwise I wouldn't understand it, not after all she'd done for them."

He sounded pathetically relieved by the thin excuse I had put forward.

"Why did you sign the card with the wreath as from the 'Stepping Stones'?"

He walked across to the windows and looked out.

"Oh, that—the 'Stepping Stones'—well, that was just a little name we invented. Stepping Stones to a fresh start, that sort of thing. Just a nickname for ourselves."

"She died near some stepping-stones in Pompeii."

"Did she? Odd coincidence. Were the police getting anywhere by the time you left?"

"I doubt it."

I was wondering whether to tell him of the things which had happened to me. I heard him say, without looking round:

"If this damned young chap doesn't come in the next half-hour I'll be gone. I suppose I could leave the guns with the porter downstairs and put a note on the door. Young chaps these days seem to have no idea of punctuality."

I decided not to do so. He was leaving in half-an-hour, leaving the country and, as I saw it, the danger in London which surrounded him.

I thought: let him go in peace, unworried and undisturbed. Let the old boy go and live in the sun in comfort and at ease, for his last years.

He turned and came back to the fireplace and knocked his pipe out in the grate, and immediately began to refill it from his worn pouch.

"You know," he said thoughtfully, "that woman was a bit of a saint, in some ways."

"Was she?" I said. "Was she indeed?"

"I'll tell you why. You could use it, you could put it in your book or article or whatever you're writing. She helped these types though it must have gone right against the grain."

"Because of what she had suffered at the hands of crooks? She and her parents and her husband and so on?"

"You know about that?"

"They told me at the hotel."

"She thought that nothing was too bad for the average criminal. You should have heard her sometimes—hang 'em, flog 'em, lock 'em up for life, all that. It was a bit extreme, really. I think she did this work as a sort of sop to her conscience. Psychological, you know," he added solemnly. "That's what it was, in some way or other, psychological—not that I believe much in that sort of damned nonsense."

He was at his pipe again, clouds of smoke billowing round his face.

"God knows what I'll have to smoke in Portugal," he muttered.

Then, reverting, he said: "She was a great disciplinarian with herself, too, mind you. I believe she took up this work like some people have a cold bath in the morning—unpleasant, but good for the soul."

"Do you have a cold bath in the morning?" I asked.

I wanted something to say, to keep the conversation going, to keep his mind off the time and the thought of last-minute things to do.

I was afraid he was going to look at his watch and say, well, would I excuse him, and I didn't want to excuse him, because what might seem a simple theory to anybody reading about it afterwards was not at all simple to me at that time, and in that place; and edging up to it as I was, with a feeling of astonishment and excitement, it was not easy to sort out a number of questions which occurred to me. I heard him say:

"Do I take a cold bath in the morning. No, of course I don't take a cold bath in the morning. Damned nonsense, if you ask me. Do you?"

"No, I don't."

"I should think not indeed."

"These jobs she found for them," I asked. "What sort of jobs were they, in what fields?"

Now, in fact, he did glance at his watch.

"In what fields? Oh, I forget now—engineering, chemicals, building, ship-repair firms—that sort of thing."

"Catering?"

"Catering? Oh, yes, that, of course. Catering and the hotel business."

"Could you give me any examples of how they have got on?"

"Oh, I couldn't give you any names, anything which would enable you to identify them, that would be out of the question. And now, I'm afraid, if you'll excuse me—"

"I'm not asking for names," I said rapidly, "just sort of examples."

He began to move slowly towards the drawing-room door.

"Well, I think I can tell you this, without being unethical—I know of one assistant manager of a big engineering firm who is, well, one of our boys, so to speak! And an English export manager in Switzerland, and a hotel manager in the south of France, and one in Italy, and one here—in England, itself—on the south coast, though she's a manageress."

He stopped by the door and looked at me knowingly.

"She always told me how they were getting on. There were no secrets of that sort between Lucy Dawson and me," said this simple soldier.

I had to go now.

There were other questions I would have liked to put to him, but he wanted me off the premises. I followed him to the front door, listening to him muttering about his guns and unpunctuality.

Yet as we were about to say good-bye, and after I had thanked him, he unwittingly provided what seemed to me to be the main startling clue to the whole affair.

I remember he laughed heartily and said:

"It's a good job we were all honest people, eh? Lucy Dawson and me and Caroline Gray!"

"Caroline Gray?"

"Lucy started it up alone, but afterwards a woman called Caroline Gray helped her. After she had retired, that is. She used to be Deputy Governor in one of the women's prisons. Great judge of character! Helped Lucy a lot. Became great buddies. But as I say, good job we were honest! What a chance for blackmail, eh?"

I laughed, too. It was one of the most unamused laughs I have ever given.

So we parted, laughing mutually, and I wished him a happy and healthy life.

⁓

I walked slowly from Benton House and all the way to Kensington, thinking of how Lucy Dawson and her family had suffered at the hands of criminals and how she felt towards them.

Above all I thought of the revenge she had chosen.

It was frightening in its long-term cruelty, just because of the deceptive benevolence with which the trap was set.

I imagined her, tall, gracious, and gentle—and probably good-looking in those days—interviewing her victims with sympathy and understanding. Finding out by courteous probing what sort of work they were most fitted to do, in which spheres their personalities would blend most harmoniously, promising nothing at first, pointing out the difficulties, laying stress upon the need for future hard work, and above all integrity.

No doubt she would touch lightly but tactfully upon the risks to her own reputation, the dangers to her work, if her faith in the basic goodness of mankind were to be betrayed.

Then, over the years, came the periodic letters, the solicitous inquiries about what progress was being made. And Christmas cards of course, certainly Christmas cards.

Lucy Dawson—not the Lady with the Lamp, but the Lady with the Lifebelt. And attached to the Lifebelt was a Lifeline.

She never let go of it.

Attached to the lifebelt was a bill.

When you are floundering in deep waters and in peril of drowning you don't think about bills. Above all you don't think of Lucy Dawson's kind of bill.

Lucy Dawson's war of revenge against the criminal world was a long war, the more merciless because her victims were the ones who might have been salvaged, indeed were salvaged. But in her dark distorted mind there was no element of discrimination.

So, as I walked, I imagined her.

The long wait did not matter for her, for all the time she was, as it were, licking her chops before the meal. Anticipation can give as much if not more pleasure than realisation. When the fruit was ripe, she plucked it.

I wondered in what way the blackmail approach was made. Perhaps in a letter, at first, to prepare the ground: *"Being acquainted, as by experience you undoubtedly are, with the type of work in which I am interested, it has been suggested to me that you will probably be willing to subscribe to our funds. I would not, of course, approach you in this way if I did not think that you were sympathetic to our aims. Perhaps I might telephone you one day, or we might meet, in order to decide upon the amount which you will, I feel certain, wish to give annually to such a deserving cause."*

Nothing threatening.

Merely the implied certainty that there would be no refusal.

How much did she take? Five, ten, twenty per cent of their salaries? Was it all in cash, or was it in cash and kind? Did Bardoni pay her entire hotel bill, when she stayed there under the fiction that she liked to pay the manager direct? Did the others do likewise? What of Miss Brett and the Bower Hotel? Did she pay Miss

Brett a certain sum, and order that unattractive woman to make up the difference?

What of Mrs. Gray? No distorted mind there. Just money. What was her cut?

The questions raced through my mind, and although I could not expect to find an answer to these particular ones, I was convinced that I was on the right track.

I thought I had the answer to the whole thing: Mrs. Dawson had been running a long-term blackmail racket, and somebody had revolted at last, and killed her at Pompeii.

I thought it was as simple as that.

By the time I had arrived back at the flat I was still sure I was right. As a small check, I telephoned the International Seamen's Widows' and Orphans' Fund, on whose behalf she wrote so many letters, according to what Mrs. Dacey had told me at the Bower Hotel.

I was not surprised to learn they had never heard of her. She was too busy, I thought, writing to her victims, to bother about seamen's widows and orphans.

But the centre core of the problem, the big, menacing question mark still remained unsolved.

I understood the minor obstructions I had encountered, the attempts to dissuade me from my investigations made by Bardoni. Poor old Bardoni, I thought, and almost softened towards him in spite of his eyes hacked out of chunks of oak. What crime had he committed in his youth? What toll did he pay to Mrs. Dawson, how long had it been going on? Had she known that Juliet was his daughter when Stanley and Elaine Bristow visited his hotel to carry out their warped experiment?

I could understand his fears all right. I could understand those of the unloveable Constance Brett, whose whole life was bound up in her job at the Bower Hotel.

Mrs. Gray was different. How much did she know of the victims, and was she planning to take over the racket?

It was at this point that my thinking faltered.

These people were tiddlers, swimming around fearful and wide-eyed, afraid of anything which might disturb the calm patch of water they had reached after much toil and trouble. I recalled the thoughts I had had in the taxi as I hastened to interview Colonel Pearson.

So who was the Big Cat, the powerful one, the one with power, riches and organisational ability, the one who was cool and cautious, who preferred to gain his ends by fear, if he could, rather than risk a killing, but who, nevertheless, had certainly killed poor Bunface?

I am sometimes a slow thinker; and then again, sometimes my thoughts can become so complicated and involved that I cannot see the obvious, even when it is almost crying out to be recognised.

But now, with a jolt, I saw that which should have been long since apparent to me.

Hitherto, I had linked the petty obstructions of Bardoni and Constance Brett with the campaign against me, regarding them as stemming from the same motives, lumping the Big Fish with the tiddlers.

Now I began to see the truth, or at least part of it.

The tiddlers were afraid for *themselves.*

The Big Cat, the Great Predator, was afraid *for the organisation.*

Lucy Dawson's racket had been taken over. The motive for her murder was not that of a blackmail victim who had reached the end of his tether.

The motive was money.

A going concern.

Vast profit and no capital risks.

No risks of any kind, if the cards were played right.

A gangster take-over, possibly originating in Italy, possibly not. I wondered whether they had offered her a cut or a partnership.

But they had misjudged her. Knowing nothing of her sad past, having no inkling of the secret, dark corners of a tragic, inhibited, and unforgiving soul, they could not see that to take this thing from her would be like removing the mainspring from a clock.

The last rendezvous at Pompeii had been the final attempt.

I could imagine her saying, in effect, "Over my dead body."

And so it was. So it was, indeed.

I was very delighted and relieved by this theory, as I opened the street door leading to my flat. The dominating emotion was relief.

Some things, some tricks they had played, still baffled me, but I no longer had any lingering doubts at all about my mental stability. Nor, frankly, had I much fear. I was just faced with a bunch of crooks.

I could handle a bunch of crooks.

Thus I let myself in, overwhelmed by my own brilliance, dazzled by my own acumen, and infinitely glad that whatever anybody else thought I had discovered the key to the current problem.

There proved to be a grain of truth in my new theory. A very small grain.

Otherwise it was totally wrong, like all my thoughts and actions in this calamitous affair.

~~~~~~

Still, there you are, as dapper Colonel Pearson would have said. You can only do your best.

You can only bumble along the jungle-skirted paths, and, if the crackle of twigs alarms you, you can say it is only a wild pig, not exactly harmless, but capable of being repulsed.

If you hear the slither of bodies, and the sound continues with you, then of course it is a different matter. But you can only hitch your spear forward and hope for the best. You can console yourself with the thought that more peasants get through than not.

It can, however, be fatal, even in this modern day and age, not to keep your eyes open and your spear ready, and to think that it is always the other peasant who is clawed down.

Mind you, it probably always will be the other peasant, until one day the other peasant is you.

CHAPTER 10

So I let myself in, and on the mat inside the door was another buff envelope, which for a second I thought was a bill from my garage; but it was the middle of the month, not the beginning, and I suppose I realised as I stooped down to pick it up that it was another note. I opened it there and then.

The message, civil enough, was couched in the same intolerably pompous language as its predecessor:

> You appear to have in your possession a red
> pelargonium, commonly, though incorrectly called
> geranium. Observation has indicated that this potted
> plant is currently in your kitchen.
> Should you wish to accede at any time to the
> very reasonable request already made to you, it is
> suggested that you place this plant upon the window

sill of your front room, where it will be readily noticed from the street.

It is regretted that up to now your general reaction appears to have been of a negative nature. You
will certainly appreciate that the present activities are
time and money wasting and it is unfortunately true
to say that unless a more positive reaction, as indicated above, becomes apparent by seven o'clock tomorrow morning, some signal mark of displeasure
will be manifested, either against you personally, or
against your fiancée, Miss Juliet Bristow, either immediately or in the near future. This it would be mutually desirable to avoid.

As you appear to be a comparatively late riser,
you may like to place the plant in the window this
evening, or even now, should you so wish.

The note was dated that day. It had been typed upon my machine, using my typing paper and enclosed in one of my envelopes.
But on leaving the flat I had taken certain precautions.

I went upstairs and examined the mortice lock. The thin wafer
of tissue paper was still in place, and when I let myself in the faint
dusting of salt just inside the door was undisturbed.

I sat down and read the note again.

For the second time within a few hours, I realised how alone
one can feel when there is no police force to whom one can effectively appeal for support. The last time I had called on them I could
not even produce the note. This time I would have a note.

"Look," I could say, "I've had another note. Here it is! It's getting serious! You'll have to do something."

"Oh, yes, sir?" they'd say, kindly and avuncular. "What's the
trouble this time? Let's have a look at it, shall we?"

So I would give it to them, and they'd say:

"And was this one typed on your machine, Mr. Compton—like
the last one?"

"Yes, it was," I'd say.

"So somebody's been in your flat again, have they, sir?"

"No, they haven't. That's the point. Between the time I left the flat this morning, and my return to find this note, nobody had been inside. I put a piece of tissue paper in the mortice lock, and sprinkled some salt just inside the front door, and they were undisturbed. So nobody's been inside, see?"

"You sprinkled salt all over your own carpet and stuck a bit of bumph in the lock?"

"Yes, I did."

"And what do you want us to do, sir? Come and sweep up the salt?"

In the end I would lose my temper, and that would confirm their views of me. I couldn't face it.

But I knew now a little more, a fraction more, of what I was up against, and it was not reassuring. This campaign was planned by somebody who had acquired a knowledge of my character. It had been planned step by step in advance. Whoever had gone into my flat, and typed the first note, had at the same time typed the second.

They knew my first instinct would be to resist.

They guessed they would need the second note.

Maybe they had typed a third at the same time, even more peremptory, a very final warning, but I didn't think so. They wouldn't keep it up indefinitely, not the pressure at its present intensity, with its cost in money and time.

The crunch was bound to come soon.

One of us was going to take decisive action.

Looking back, I can see the matter depended upon three national characteristics in my make-up: Irish bloody-mindedness, Boer tenacity, English coolness and instinct for compromise.

The make-up was two to one in favour of a fight.

I wonder if they knew it. They had assessed the character presented to the world: the happy-go-lucky Irish streak, the good-natured Dutch streak, the clinically cool English streak and on the surface the assessment looked promising. But I wondered if they had examined deeply, individually and separately, the underlying implications of the three separate blood streams.

If so, they should have known that if you push your luck too far, with either the Irish or the Dutch, you'll get an explosion of unreasoning and unexpected violence. The English react in the same way, but it takes longer because they are more calculating.

I thought of the threat to Juliet, but I dismissed it as bluff.

They must have known that if they killed Juliet nothing would ever stop me.

Suddenly I felt the explosion building up inside me.

I was fed up with the whole damned boiling. I wasn't going to be pushed around by a crowd of bloody gangsters engaged in a take-over bid.

I would see them to hell before I knuckled under. If it was to be one man against the organisation, well, then, so be it. They could go and jump in the bloody Thames. Ah, me—brave words.

The anger swirled round and round in my stomach. I could feel the pulses in my forehead beating rapidly. Imaginary dialogue between me and them flashed through my mind, and still the fury churned up inside me, and there were more brave words.

I got up out of my chair and walked to the windows which looked out upon Stratford Road, and opened one of the windows and stood by it, and tore the latest note into pieces, and crumpled the pieces together, and tossed them down into the street, thereby, incidentally, risking a Summons for littering the highway.

Next, the furious defiance still upon me, I went into the kitchen.

The red geranium stood on a coarse cast blue-green saucer I had bought in the south of France. I snatched the plant from the saucer, and went to the kitchen waste bin. It had a lid which you raised by pressing a knob with your foot, and this I did.

I lifted my arm to hurl the plant into the bin, but I didn't do so.

It was the English streak, the practical, dispassionate, despicable, cool, god-damned-awful, reasonable, cautious, sensible, calculating, unloveable trait which conquered an Empire and yielded it without much fuss when the time was ripe, which now held me back, whispering insidiously that there was no point in destroying a good plant.

What harm to keep it in the kitchen?

I replaced it upon its horrid saucer, and so it stood, invisible from the street, but still in being, a green and red testimony to an inherited Anglo-Saxon reluctance to burn any boats in the rear.

I went round for supper at the Bristows' that evening.

CHAPTER 11

I have purposely refrained from describing the preparations for the wedding, now only three days distant, because for those who are not involved nothing could be more boring. If it comes to that, nothing is more boring for the bridegroom. All he is anxious to do is to marry as quickly and neatly as possible, and get off on his honeymoon, leaving all the flap behind for other people to clear up, and, incidentally, pay for.

Stanley Bristow had naturally been in his element, organising, amending, and confirming every detail, such as the hire of cars, the time of their arrival at the house, the estimated time of arrival at the church, the estimated time of departure from the church after the ceremony, the invitations, the music, the printing, the photographers, the champagne, the catering, and the flowers.

This, one felt, was his finest hour.

In so far as the atmosphere was concerned when I went round that evening, I can say that it was determinedly cheerful.

I recalled the little group I had seen on the doorstep the previous night—Stanley, the Inspector, and the sergeant—tying up the loose ends, checking my statement as far as they could, eliminating me from the list of people who could conceivably have killed poor Bunface.

To put it brutally, it seemed that Stanley and Elaine Bristow were now reconciled to the fact that Juliet was going to marry a man who was still suffering from the after-effects of a car crash, but had doubtless come to the conclusion that to postpone the wedding would be inconvenient and embarrassing.

I believed, and still believe, that Juliet's feelings were different. She thought she was marrying a mentally sick man, but one whom she loved and could nurse back to mental health. Poor old Juliet.

I noticed this bright atmosphere at the start. There was the exaggerated enthusiasm about the wedding presents which had arrived, the optimistic prognostications about the weather, the certainty that the bridesmaids would appreciate their ghastly, tawdry presents, which, according to Elaine Bristow, looked as though they had cost twice as much as they had done, though privately I didn't agree.

All three chattered incessantly about everything except that which was uppermost in their minds. I prayed along with them until after dinner. Then I said:

"I had another threatening note today. Like the other one."

Juliet was not in the sitting-room. Elaine Bristow was, but she muttered something and left me alone with Stanley.

Stanley was drinking a glass of brandy. He put his glass down on a small table by his chair.

"Let's have a look at it, old boy," he said, in his eager, snuffly tone. "I think you ought to take it to the police, old boy, I really do. Practical jokes are practical jokes, but this is getting a bit thick, old boy, it really is."

He gazed at me with his exophthalmic goitre eyes and held out his hand. I suppose he thought I was going to fish about in my pocket and slap it into his outstretched palm.

"I tore it up," I said.

"Tore it up?"

"You know as well as I do, by now, that it was no good taking it to the police. You know what they think, don't you?"

"I don't know what the police think, old boy," he muttered evasively. "How should I know what they think?"

I felt the anger begin to churn around in my stomach again; not as intensely as before, but enough to be going on with.

"They were here last night, weren't they? Checking?"

"They called here, yes."

"Checking my movements?"

"They asked a few questions, yes, they did, they asked a few questions, old boy. Just routine stuff. Nothing to worry about."

"Nothing for whom to worry about? Nothing for them to worry about? Nothing for you to worry about? Is that it? Good old them, good old you!"

I was sitting on a settee on the left side of the fireplace, and watched him get up and walk to the grate, and stand with his back to it, tall, and droopy, and ineffectual, staring down awkwardly at me.

The door opened and Juliet came in.

"I was just saying that I had had another note, Juliet, like the other one."

"But he tore it up," murmured Stanley Bristow. "He tore it up, for some reason, so he can't show it to us."

"Never mind," said Juliet cheerfully, and went out carrying an early morning tea-set given me by a cousin. It was egg yellow, and the cups and tea-pot were square. This cousin and I never liked each other.

She gave me a smile as she closed the door. It was a sort of open, understanding, maternal smile. It didn't suit her.

I preferred her slow, discreet smiles which made you want to ask what the hell she was laughing at, and the secretive sidelong looks, and the withdrawn manner. I preferred the Italian streak, even if it did come from old Bardoni, rather than the open Anglo-Saxon stuff. But I was glad of the smile, and glad of the way she had received me. She had forgotten, or pretended to have forgotten, the bitterness of my parting words the previous night.

Stanley and I sat and looked at each other in silence for a few seconds, then he cleared his throat and said:

"Elaine and I have been thinking, old boy—"

"I know what you've been thinking, all right. So has Juliet," I said. "In some ways I don't blame you. I can't produce any proof. I would if I could, but I can't, but I think I'm beginning to see the answer."

"Beginning to see the answer?"

"Vaguely. Possibly."

I told him about the letter in the newspaper, and my visit to old Colonel Pearson, and the theory I had built up as a result of his casual, parting remark.

Stanley listened attentively, sometimes sipping his brandy and saying: "Ah, crooks," or "Blackmail, eh?" or "Gangsters, what?"

Just as I finished, the door opened and Juliet came back with Elaine Bristow.

Stanley said:

"James says he now knows the answer to all this nonsense. It's a blackmail racket, he says. This old woman, Mrs. Dawson, she helped crooks to get jobs and then later in life she blackmailed them. And now she's been bumped off by gangsters who've taken over the racket. James has got the whole story from a colonel who was a prison governor, and used to supply names to Mrs. Dawson. How's that, Elaine? What about that, Juliet? That explains it, doesn't it? Damned serious matter, eh?"

I would have been deceived, I would have thought his enthusiasm was genuine, if I hadn't glanced at his eyes and seen they were lacking in all lustre. He was forcing himself to smile eagerly, and forcing tones of interest into his voice, but his protruding eyes were like those of a dead fish.

"What's James got to do with it?" asked Elaine patiently.

"How does James come into it?" asked Juliet.

Stanley looked at them without blinking.

"James says they're afraid of what he'll discover. The gangsters want him to lay off, that's how James comes into it."

"This man, this colonel, must go to the police and tell them what he knows," said Elaine Bristow in a tired voice. "You must get him along to the police, Stanley, get him along tomorrow, this is important."

"I will, and James can come with me. This might clear the whole matter up. I'll go along and see him tomorrow, and James'll come with me, won't you."

I couldn't understand this suggestion.

"It's not as simple as that," I said hopelessly. "You've jumped to conclusions. I didn't say this was what *had* happened. I didn't say that at all, all I said was that this was what might have happened. And even that was based on a joking remark by Colonel Pearson. Anyway, it's too late. You can't see him, he's gone."

"Gone?" said Juliet.

"What do you mean, he's gone?" asked Stanley.

"He's emigrated. Gone to Portugal. He left this morning."

"Gone? Suddenly? Just sort of flittered away? Like that?"

I saw this fool's eyes come to life. He was back to square one. You get to a point where the jangled nerves won't stand any more.

"You bloody well think I'm nuts, don't you?" I suddenly shouted. "You think the whole thing is a creation of my mind? Just because I can't produce a snapshot of the man calling himself Sergeant Matthews, or the messages, or a recording of the man on the 'phone, you think I'm just a bit barmy—well, don't you? Just because this is something which you've never come across in your safe humdrum life, you think it can't exist. You make me sick, and I don't mean mentally sick, though it may come to that, by God!"

I saw Elaine Bristow suddenly swell and turn pink. She said:

"Stanley was only trying to help, James! Stanley was going to make a suggestion, as a matter of fact."

"Oh, indeed? What sort of suggestion?" I asked acidly.

"Even before this last—well, your last outburst, he was going to suggest that, well—" She began to falter.

"I know a man," said Stanley Bristow unexpectedly loudly. "I know a damned good man in Harley Street."

I looked at him and saw that he had gone as pink as Elaine.

"How nice for you."

"Listen, old boy," he went on, snuffling the words out rapidly, almost incoherently, "there's nothing to be worried about, nothing at all, and nothing to be ashamed of, and we're not suggesting anything for the moment, but later, perhaps after the wedding and the honeymoon, we thought, Elaine and I, that is, we thought that perhaps if you had—what shall we say?—a good overhaul by this chap, it would do no harm. See what I mean? Not psycho-analysis, or any nonsense like that. Knew him in the Army, splendid chap, full of common sense. Not now. Later. And anyway, perhaps when you and Juliet get back from the south of France, we can think again. Perhaps these—these gangsters—perhaps they'll have stopped persecuting you by then, see what I mean?"

He stopped. The mumbling contradictions in his speech didn't occur to him. Elaine looked at him almost admiringly. She seemed to think he had put it over rather well.

Then they both looked at me, and Juliet, who had been pretending to read an evening paper, gave me one of her sidelong glances without raising her head from the paper.

I got up and walked over to Stanley with my glass.

"Can I have another brandy?"

"Of course you can, old boy," he said, though not very willingly. He was probably thinking that hot, sweet tea is better for cases of shock. He poured out one of the smallest tots I've seen. I raised my glass.

"Here's to the Doctor, and I hope he can swim, because as far as I'm concerned he can go and jump in the river. Thanks all the same."

There was another awkward silence.

"I'm sorry you take it like that, old boy."

"Stanley was only trying to help," said Elaine.

"I know," I said, and sighed. "Oh, God, don't I know it! But Elaine, this Colonel Pearson exists—there's his letter in the paper! And I saw him this morning."

"I'm sure you did, dear," said Elaine.

"It's a pity he's gone," muttered Stanley. "That's all."

"Why? Why is it a pity? All he did was to spark off the blackmail idea in my mind."

"He's right, Elaine." He glanced quickly at her. "All the Colonel did was to spark off this blackmail idea. Just as a joke. He wouldn't have believed it, see what I mean? Anyway, we can't see him. So it's no good crying over spilt milk."

"What spilt milk? What good would it have done you to see him?" I said angrily. As I spoke I banged my glass of brandy down on the marble chimney piece. The thin goblet shattered and the remains of the brandy lay in a small pool on the marble.

"I'm sorry," I murmured, "I'm sorry I broke your glass."

"It's all right, old boy," said Stanley. He watched Elaine grab a shovel and hearth brush and sweep up the mess.

Suddenly, from the settee, Juliet said:

"I want to have a word with Jamie. We'll go out for a stroll."

But Elaine said, over her shoulder, "Don't bother, darling, Stanley and I are going to bed anyway."

"Bed?" said Stanley. "It's a bit early, isn't it? Anyway, old boy, what was in this last message you say you had?"

"It's not a question of a message I *said* I had, it's a message I *did* have."

"Yes, well, all right, old boy—what did it say?"

"Much the same as before," I said sulkily. "Except that it said that if I agreed to their demands I should place a red geranium on my window sill."

"A red geranium?"

"Yes, a red geranium."

"Have you got a red geranium?"

"Of course I've got a bloody red geranium," I flared up. "It's in my damned kitchen! As they well know."

Juliet got up from the settee. Stanley took the hint, and moved to the door. Elaine followed him. At the door Stanley stopped and said:

"Well, there you are, old boy! Stick the geranium on your window sill—and then they'll all go away, won't they?—they'll disappear, all these gangsters that are after you."

He went out, followed by his over-ripe, shoddy wife. I think I can be permitted to describe her like that, even in print, in view of what happened later, just as I have been frank about Stanley.

But I stopped him before he had shut the door and said:

"That's not the point. You wouldn't understand this, perhaps, but it's important to me."

He paused with his hand on the door knob, and stared down at me.

"What's important to you, old boy?"

"It's the individual, that's what's important, it's a question of whether the individual can survive when he's pitted against the organisation, that's what matters, that's what matters to me, that's why I'm being so bloody-minded—it's not a question of whether the individual gets submerged in the State, it's something far more primitive—it's a question of whether the individual—me, in this case—has a bloody chance at all against the jungle these days, whether it's a State jungle or any other kind of modern jungle. The peasant had a chance in the old days, not much, but just a chance, but has he now, Stanley?"

Elaine had gone along the passage, Stanley Bristow stood looking at me blankly.

"It's all right," I said. "Forget it. You don't understand."

"Of course I understand, old boy. You want to prove you can stand on your own feet. Quite right, too!"

I guessed it was silly to have submerged him in a stream of words and ideas. I imagined he was thinking that it was bad enough to have me suffering from an imaginary persecution, without having me build abstruse theories upon it.

"That's right," I said hastily. "Well, good night."

"Good night, old boy."

I helped him to close the door in case he came back at me. I couldn't bear any more of him. Then I turned and saw Juliet, and in a way I was pleased and in a way I was shocked.

She was standing stiffly by the fireplace. All the superficial brightness had gone out of her.

The fear was back in her eyes.

"You don't want to worry," I said uneasily.

I went to put my arms around her, but she drew back.

"What's the matter?" I said, as though I didn't know.

"I now think it's true," she said, staring at me with big, frightened, dark eyes. "I think what you said is true, I think you're up against something—some big criminal thing. It didn't make sense till you saw Colonel Pearson, but it does now."

"Maybe I'm right, and maybe I'm wrong," I said, as lightly as I could. "Come on, cheer up."

I put an arm round her and kissed her. She didn't resist, but her lips were cold. She said:

"If I never ask you to do another thing, will you do this one thing for me?"

"The geranium?"

She nodded. I turned away.

"No," I said. "No darling. I can't. Not even for you."

I watched the tears welling up in her eyes.

"It's not just the story now. It's not just a dislike of being pushed around. I've just got to prove something."

"What?" she said evenly, but a second later I heard her sob.

To my astonishment, I heard myself echoing, in some part, Stanley Bristow's words.

"That if he's in the right, or at any rate not in the wrong, then a man can stand on his own feet, even these days against the organisation. It doesn't mean much, I suppose, to most people. But I'm a bit keen on the idea."

When we parted she was more cheerful. If she wasn't, she pretended to be. I didn't tell her that her name had been mentioned in the last message. I didn't truthfully think it was more than bluff. I suppose it was criminally wrong of me.

CHAPTER 12

There was nothing in my letter box when I retained to my flat, except the evening paper. I glanced through it before I went to bed. On one of the inside pages, a brief news item said that the woman murdered in Paradise Lane had now been identified as a spinster, aged forty-seven, called Mavis Battersby, of 247 Furleigh Road, London, N.W.1.

It didn't seem to matter.

To me she would always be Poor Bunface, not Mavis Battersby. The real name meant nothing, does not mean anything now, and never will mean anything. I thought, think, and always will think, that she was killed because she knew a little too much, and because she was on the verge of cracking up.

When I undressed I went into the kitchen to get a glass of water. I always have a glass of water by my bed at night. Not a plastic tooth mug filled with water, but a real glass. Water tastes better in a glass.

I looked at the geranium in its pot on the window sill.

Its best summer blooms were past, but it still had one or two smaller autumnal flowers. It was leggy and some of the leaves had turned brown round the edges. I would cut it back in due course, and give it the minimum of water during the winter months, and next year it would flourish again.

Suddenly I felt extraordinarily tired; not physically tired, but spiritually exhausted. The temptation to lift the plant, take a few steps out of the kitchen and put it on the living-room window was irresistible.

I had felt all along that because the threat was seriously and efficiently operated, I could completely rely upon obtaining relief by carrying out their instructions. I was not faced with shifty little crooks whose word could not be trusted. This was something bigger; and, because it was coolly calculated, and, if my theory was correct, meant a great deal financially to the operators, then their terms would be honoured.

I turned away from the plant, and ran the tap to make sure the water would be cold, and as I waited, the feeling of spiritual exhaustion left me and was replaced by something more dangerous. It was a feeling of apathy. Exhaustion is a positive thing. You are conscious of it. You can try to do something about it.

Apathy is the negation of all effort and all emotion. Apathy means that if there is no way of avoiding action, then you take the easiest line.

I suddenly wanted to be left in peace.

Subtle voices spoke to me, pointing out that I was not engaged upon a crusade to save a large cross-section of humanity, but indulging in stubbornness and personal pride. Blackmail gangs always existed and always would, and the victims had only themselves to blame. Anyway, I couldn't ever prove anything, and the police were not interested, and why should I be?

The subtlest voice of all argued in favour of a temporary surrender, until the heat had died down. This voice was a very crafty one indeed, and went into some detail.

The burden of its argument was that the people were intelligent enough to know that I was certainly not the only crime writer who would be interested, at some time or other, in the Pompeii murder. Although the Italian police might be content with current facts and clues, somebody, some day, would write the case up in great detail and with a full background. A black-out could not be maintained indefinitely. Therefore, the voice whispered, the black-out was being imposed for a limited period for some special purpose. So why not lay off now, and return to the fray later?

I picked up the geranium, and went out of the kitchen, feeling no sensation of defeat.

I turned right, into the bedroom, and put the glass on my bedside table, and went into the living-room, carrying the plant. The curtains were drawn, and I put the pot on the sill, preparatory to pulling the curtains aside.

But it wasn't any use.

I remember I stood staring at it, thinking: there you are, boyo, on your hideous green saucer, representing the victory of the organised predators over the peasant who chooses to walk the trails alone. He thinks the Tribe can protect him, and sometimes it can, and sometimes it can't, but it ought to be able to; and the more times it proves it can, the better for all peasants, but the peasants have got to lend a hand, they've got to fight back themselves, they've got to show willing, and if a peasant shows willing, in this day and age, then the peasant ought to be able to win through against the predators. He damned well ought to win through. Maybe he gets clawed down by that lot who slither along the jungle undergrowth beside him. Maybe he dies, and maybe he goes on, but he's got to have a crack at it, God damn and blast everything and everybody, he's got to fight back, because if he doesn't bloody well fight back as an individual peasant, then the whole bloody Tribe is lost, because the individuals make the Tribe, it's not the Tribe which makes the individuals, and damn all organised predators, and long live the peasant, I thought.

So it wasn't any use, and I walked back into the kitchen and put the geranium in its accustomed place, and then went into the living-room and drew the curtains aside, so that by seven-thirty next morning my decision would be clear.

I went to bed, and slept reasonably well, and at seven-forty the

next morning the telephone rang, and I naturally guessed who it
was before I had lifted the receiver.

~~~~

The voice was just the same as the first time, but he had now
adopted a polite, but chilly tone.

"Well, now, this is most disappointing, isn't it?" he said without preamble, and his voice was a sigh of regret at the intractibility
of the human race.

"Oh, go to hell!" I said.

"Tell her to wear spectacles today, and at the wedding, if she's
there," he said quickly and urgently, as though he were afraid I
might ring off, and not answer the 'phone if it rang again.

"What do you mean?" I said sharply. I felt a jolt of fear in my
stomach as sudden as an electric shock.

"What do I mean? I mean, I don't think you are taking us seriously," he said equally sharply. "That's what I mean. That's just
what I mean, that and nothing more, nothing more than I said in
the note you tore up. Got it? Remember what I said about a mark of
disfavour? Got it?"

He asked questions, but he didn't wait for a reply. He was
speaking very rapidly indeed. It now occurred to me that he
thought I might have made arrangements with the telephone au-
thorities to notify the police of all calls to me from a telephone
booth, as though he feared a police car might draw up outside his
booth at any moment.

"Seven-thirty was the deadline. Seven-thirty this morning. I've
been instructed to—"

In his haste he began to fumble for words.

"You've been instructed to do what?" I said as calmly as I
could. "What have you—"

"I've been instructed to demonstrate that we mean literally
what we say, so that—"

"Oh, for God's sake be your age," I broke in.

"Listen, I must go now, but—"

"Well, go then—I don't want to talk to you—" I said brusquely, because I couldn't resist the temptation to be rude.

"Don't suppose you do," he said quickly. "Don't suppose you wanted to in the first place. Bad luck for you, isn't it?"

Now for the first time the enamel was wearing thin. The politeness was departing. There was a quick, vicious tang to his voice.

"It's too late now," he snapped. "Too late for quite a while. But we'll be back, see? Meanwhile, you'll learn that we mean business, see? Meanwhile, get your girl to wear glasses—that's my advice. Later, if you still love her—"

"What do you mean by that?"

"What I say—mark of displeasure, see what I mean?"

"What mark of displeasure?" I said shakily, and felt the electric shock in the stomach again. "What do you mean, mark of displeasure?"

But I thought I saw what he was implying.

"I suppose you know the penalty for a razor attack?" I muttered ineffectually.

I heard him laugh.

"Nothing crude like that. We wouldn't slash her. But remember about the glasses. For her own good, see? Nothing against her personally. She's just dead unlucky. Don't want to blind her. Acid is nasty stuff when you get it in the face," he added abruptly, and I heard him replace the receiver.

I stared down at the telephone.

Now I was genuinely afraid.

Just as I had believed that if I had surrendered to their demands, Juliet and I would have gone unharmed, so now I believed without doubt that the threat to mar Juliet's magnolia skin by flinging acid in her face was a genuine one.

I began to move restlessly about the flat, and did so for an hour or more desperately trying to decide upon some sort of action. In the end, without having bathed or shaved, or had a cup of tea, though it was already nine o'clock, I went downstairs and out to my car and drove to the police station.

Whatever the cost in humiliation, I had to make one more effort, now that Juliet was involved.

Unluckily, the same alert young sergeant was on duty as when I had called previously. He not only remembered me, he even called me by my name.

"Good morning, Mr. Compton," he said pleasantly. "More trouble?"

"Is the superintendent in?"

"Ah, the superintendent?" he replied carefully. "Now he's a difficult man to pin down. And very busy, always out and about, as you can imagine. Can I give him a message?"

"I want to know if he is in," I said doggedly. "If he is, I want to see him."

He leaned across the counter and began to talk in a chummy, confidential kind of way. I think he saw himself as a cross between Dixon of Dock Green and Spencer Tracy in an old-time film.

"Look, sir, he *is* in—that's true—he *is* in, but he's got a very important conference on, see?"

"When will he be free?"

He shrugged his shoulders evasively.

"Maybe an hour, maybe much longer. You can't tell, sir."

"I'll wait. I'll sit down and wait."

"May I suggest something, sir? Why don't you just let me write down what you want to tell him, and then, maybe, when he's read it, he can get into touch with you, eh? How would that do? Save you all this waiting, eh, sir?"

He spoke in a kindly, gentle way, as one might to a very old lady suffering from mental deterioration. I had to bite back the instinct to be impatient with him. I had to remind myself that these people genuinely and reasonably thought I was suffering from a persecution complex, or at the very least some mental disturbance brought on by a car crash. There had been a few ghastly hours when I had had doubts myself. In the circumstances, he was being very patient and humane.

I nodded and pulled at my chin and felt the stubble. I don't suppose my unshaven appearance and hastily combed hair improved matters.

I remembered that the superintendent and the sergeant had

been a little rough at one point. But now I couldn't blame them either.

They had been pulled in, from the first important stages of a murder hunt, to talk to a man who appeared to be suffering from some kind of post-accident neurosis.

"All right," I said abruptly. "Tell him this. Tell the superintendent this. Tell him I've had another letter, like the previous one, but also threatening my fiancée. Tell him I've had another 'phone call, too, threatening to throw acid in her face, either today or tomorrow at my wedding. My wedding is at the Catholic Church in Baxter Street, Mayfair, at three-thirty, got it?"

"I'll tell him, sir. Don't worry."

"Tell him I want police protection."

"I'll tell him, sir," said the sergeant. "I'll tell him all that, never you fear."

"Tell him, I don't think—"

I stopped and hesitated.

"You don't think what, sir?"

"Tell him I don't think my fiancée will need police protection today, but I want it at the church tomorrow. Right?"

"I'll tell him what you say, sir."

"Thank you," I said dully. "Thank you very much."

He would pass on my request, but nothing would happen. You couldn't expect anything to happen, I thought. You couldn't expect the police to provide protection for every nut-case who thought he was being persecuted. He hadn't even asked to see the written message I had torn up.

I did not ask for protection for Juliet that day because except in a very important case, what does it amount to? A constable passing the house a little more frequently than usual? Knocking at the door a couple of times a day to see if all is in order, perhaps when the damage is done? The police station checking by 'phone when there is no one there to reply? I didn't know.

What I did know was that they couldn't detail a couple of men to follow Juliet around London on her last-minute chores.

I rang up Stanley Bristow. I had to feel that I had gone through what one might call all the paper formalities, useless though they might be.

He said he was glad I had 'phoned. He wanted to check one or two points about the speeches. When I could get a word in edgeways I said:

"Listen, Stanley, I don't want Juliet to go out by herself today."

"She's gone, old boy."

"Gone where?"

"Only to the hairdresser's, old boy, to have a perm. Why?"

I didn't trust him enough to tell him the whole facts. I didn't trust him not to go and blab them out to Juliet. I was going to tell Juliet something, but not everything. I didn't see the point in telling her everything. You can't protect yourself against an acid thrower.

He can be anywhere. He can be in a bus, or in an Underground train, or waiting at a street corner, or passing you on the pavement, and one moment you are full of the joy of life, and the next the searing burning fluid is over your face, and your skin is ruined, and if it gets into your eyes your sight may be gone for ever, and that is that, and it's no good talking then about police protection, or wearing glasses to protect your eyes.

"Forget it," I said, "there's nothing one can do about it today."

Nor was there. If the police couldn't protect her, then Stanley Bristow couldn't. In the close-knit circle of a wedding, it was possible; in the normal run of the day, there was no chance.

"Somebody rang up again," I went on. "The usual thing, the usual threat."

He didn't say anything for a moment. Then he said soothingly:

"Don't worry, old boy, don't worry at all! Everything's going to be all right. You mustn't worry, see? Take it easy. Don't overdo it, and above all have a good night's rest. You've got a busy day tomorrow."

Later, Juliet had lunch with me. It was our last meeting alone before the wedding. She was quiet, paler than usual and jumpy. I supposed that fool Stanley had said something.

"Looking forward to tomorrow, darling?" I said half-way through the meal. A silly question.

She didn't look up from her plate when she answered.

"I'm dreading it," she said. "You've asked me, and I've told you. I'll be glad when it's over."

She saw my dismayed look.

"It's not that I don't love you. It's because I do."

"What's Stanley been saying?" I asked angrily.

"Nothing much."

"Stanley's always exaggerating."

"Not always."

"Nothing's changed," I said. "You must believe that. Everything is as it was. See?"

It was a flagrant lie, but I was appalled. The wedding was supposed to be a joyous day, and I saw the fragrance slipping away. Whatever was or was not to happen, I wanted her to go to her wedding with happiness.

"How long is it all to go on?" she asked sadly.

"Not long now, darling. I know that."

"How long?" she insisted.

I searched my mind for an answer.

"Only till we get back from the honeymoon."

"You don't know that."

"I do. This sort of thing can't go on."

"And if we don't get back? If one of us doesn't get back?"

"We'll get back all right," I said. "Once we're off, we'll get back all right. Don't worry about that. Don't worry about that for one moment."

My heart ached as I looked at her magnolia skin, wondering if we would, in fact, get off, or whether she would be lying in hospital with her face swathed in bandages.

⌒

I am rather a solitary walker, with few intimate friends. I had had to scratch round a bit for a best man for the wedding. In the end, a chap called Gerald Bailey agreed to do the job. We had worked together on a magazine at one period, and had kept up a desultory friendship ever since. I didn't have the usual stag party the night before, but I had to give Gerald a good dinner. It was the least I could do in exchange for the morning suit he would have to hire for the occasion.

But before I met him I called in at the Bristows' for a final word with Juliet. I couldn't delay it any longer, and in due course I said:

"Do me a favour, will you? You know I love you in glasses. Will you wear your glasses tomorrow, darling?"

She looked at me in astonishment.

"Wear my glasses? I don't need to wear my glasses."

"I know you don't need to, I just asked if you would."

"Why?"

"Because you look pretty in them."

"I shouldn't think anybody else thinks so."

"You're not marrying anybody else."

She didn't take me seriously, of course, and laughed.

"You'll have plenty of time to see me in them later."

"Please wear your glasses," I said. "Do please wear them, sweetheart, just for my sake. Will you?"

She must have noted the urgency in my voice. She looked at me, and I saw a flicker of fear reappear in her eyes.

"Why?" she asked again.

"Just because I love you in them."

She didn't ask any more. She guessed that it would be useless. Behind her quiet manner her quick brain could seize an unspoken thought, she sensed subterfuge, and yet she knew when it was useless to press a point.

"I'll see," she said, and would promise no more.

But I wondered if she *would* see, if she wore no glasses. Suddenly I broke, and cast aside my resolution.

"Juliet," I said. "Juliet, listen to me."

"What?" she said.

The flicker of fear had become a bar across her beautiful eyes.

"What I've done, I've done and whether I did right or wrong, doesn't matter now. For the time being I can't undo it. I want you to protect yourself in every way."

She looked at me thoughtfully.

"Including my eyes?"

"Well, yes, including your eyes."

"Against what?"

I hesitated a moment.

"People might throw things," I said at last. "You never know they might throw something."

"Protect my face and my eyes?" she said slowly. "And to some extent my clothes?"

I didn't say anything.

I saw the flash of naked terror though she tried to hide it, and wished I had kept quiet after all. I didn't think she would reach exactly the right conclusion so quickly.

I wasn't big enough to take upon myself the burden of responsibility. She should have at least arrived happy for her wedding.

In the event, she arrived both fearful and unprotected. Doubtless, Elaine Bristow played a part in the matter of the spectacles, but I think it was mostly vanity.

CHAPTER 13

The church we were married in was small and unpretentious. It had been built as a chapel for a Roman Catholic ambassador in penal times, and, from the outside, had the look of a disused factory. This was an intended effect. The façade was a camouflage to hide the church and protect it against eighteenth-century anti-popery riots.

Gerald Bailey drove me to the church. I suppose he attributed my tenseness to the usual nervousness of bridegrooms. He dropped me at the door and drove off to park the car somewhere.

Inside, the church looked warm and welcoming, the gilt and blue of the gallery gleaming in the light of the candles. On the steps of the altar were two huge urns of gold and white chrysanthemums. Elaine Bristow had not been mean about flowers.

Near the Lady Chapel a dozen candles were burning, and an old woman was sitting muttering, and fingering her rosary, oblivi-

ous to what was going on around her. The organist began to play a
soft wandering tune, like the background music to a film.

I did not want to go up to the altar too soon, and stood in a
side aisle in some shadows and watched the church fill up. There
were not, in fact, many guests, as weddings go, and most of them
were Juliet's.

Gerald Bailey joined me. Promptly at three-thirty I heard a car
draw up outside, and a few seconds later a car door slammed, and I
guessed it was Juliet.

Gerald and I made our way to the altar.

When I stood near the altar rails, I turned round and glanced
down the church, past the blobs of faces, to the door where Juliet
would appear.

In a seat bordering the centre aisle, and on the side occupied
by my scanty collection of guests, I caught sight of a face which
was not that of a friend or a relation, but was red, benevolent, and
vaguely familiar.

I caught a glimpse of somebody fiddling about arranging
Juliet's dress, and Stanley Bristow watching, and in those few seconds I glanced again, puzzled, at the face by the aisle.

By the time I realised it was the man who had called himself
Sergeant Matthews, Juliet was already coming through the main
door on Stanley Bristow's arm, and although she wasn't wearing
her glasses, I suddenly knew that her veil, firmly attached to her
headdress standing out stiffly from her face, white, symbolic and
protective, would be her shield.

I saw the man who called himself Matthews turn his head as
she came up the aisle. He made no movement as she passed, and she
herself, her eyes fixed ahead to the altar, passed him with no
inkling of what he represented.

Quite apart from the chains of social behaviour and custom
which kept me motionless, inhibited, reluctant to cause a scene, I
do not know to this day what practical measure I could have taken.
In law, he had a right to be sitting there, in a church open to the
public; intruding perhaps, but at the moment offending nobody.

So I watched her slowly pass him, her dress almost brushing
his arm, and felt the sweat accumulating in the palms of my hands,

because I knew that although her veil was a protection on the way in, on the way out, after the ceremony, her veil would be thrown back.

But I would be walking by her side, I thought feverishly, I would be by her side, and I could interpose my body, and I could do—something. I watched her drawing close, and thought again that I could take some action; at the first sign of a movement from him I could do something, strike, fend off, bash, kick, I could do something.

Then Juliet reached me.

She was not smiling.

She was very pale, and under the veil her large dark eyes held the bar of fear I had seen before.

She came and stood by my side, and I could see the soft cloud of her dark hair caught into unaccustomed stiffness by a knot of stephanotis. She wore a stiff silk dress, and I could hear it rustle when she moved. Her bouquet of stephanotis trembled in her hands. I smelt the strong scent of the flowers.

The priest walked down the altar steps. He was a short, red-faced man, and the lace-trimmed alb over his cassock looked odd on him.

I glanced again at Juliet, but still she didn't smile. Her lips were touched with a little colour, but otherwise her skin was as colourless as her dress. I took her hand. It was like touching a flower in the snow.

One might have thought that she knew she had just brushed past terror in the aisle, and that it was still there, behind us, as we knelt at the altar.

As with all Catholic-Protestant weddings, the service was short and simple, because a Nuptial Mass is not allowed.

Gerald Bailey handed me the ring and at the appropriate moment I said the words, "In the name of the Father, the Son and the Holy Ghost, Amen," touching each of her fingers, and with the word Amen I placed the ring on her finger, but all the time I was thinking of the walk back, down the aisle, with her veil thrown back and the man with a bottle of acid in his overcoat pocket, and I was thinking, "I'll be able to do something, something I'll be able

to do, because I know him, and I know what he plans, and fore-
warned is forearmed. So it'll be all right. Ah, God, please let it be
all right."

After the civil ceremony in the vestry, and the signing of the
Register, and the kissing and smiling, I thought again as we set out
down the aisle, "Oh God, please let it be all right. Please let me be
able to stop it."

So we set off down the aisle, and I held her very slightly back,
so that I was a fraction of a pace before her, but I needn't have
bothered, because he had gone from his seat.

I was tense and rigid and keyed up, because I thought he
might merely have changed his seat, or hidden himself elsewhere in
the church. But he hadn't.

He was nowhere in the church.

He was outside the church.

Even then he allowed the photographers to line us up. I saw
him saunter from behind a police constable of all people, a little to
the left. I had been looking at the cameramen, but I saw him all the
same. I saw him out of the corner of my eye as he suddenly quickened his step and drew nearer, and I saw him take the bottle out of
his overcoat pocket and remove the stopper.

I remember I shouted "Look out!" and flung Juliet back with
my right arm, and leaped down the three short church steps at him,
and because I had this impetus I bore him easily to the ground and
had my left hand on his right wrist, because his right hand was
holding the bottle, and with my right hand I held him on the
ground, by the throat, and looked down at him, and saw the
brown, bovine eyes looking up at me as they had looked at me
when he had called and pretended to report the fictitious complaint by poor Bunface.

I remember I gasped, "Now, you bastard!" and half choked
him.

Then I felt myself being dragged off by the policeman and Gerald Bailey.

When questioned, he said his name was Arthur Robinson of Clapham, and he had paused to watch the wedding out of curiosity.

He suffered a good deal from asthma and had been about to take a sniff of the remedy he always carried with him when I jumped at him. He showed the bottle and allowed the officer to sniff the contents.

No, he had suffered no injury from the assault, though the shock might induce an asthma attack later. No, he certainly did not wish to bring a charge against me and spoil a happy occasion. He gladly agreed that it must be a case of mistaken identity.

So he went his way, respected by all for his magnanimity.

Everybody did their best to laugh it off, at the reception. I myself could only make the lame excuse that he resembled a man who had a grudge against me and apologise to all and sundry for causing such a stupid rumpus.

But I didn't need to apologise to Juliet, and for a while the bar of fear had gone from her eyes.

We were undisturbed on our honeymoon, largely, perhaps, because we were continually on the move in the South of France. There was no threatening letter on our return.

I would have been glad to believe that we were to be left in peace, but I didn't believe it. One letter, therefore, among the pile of bills, circulars and other communications which awaited us gave me a thrill of pleasure, mixed with excitement and relief.

It was from Stanley Bristow.

He had written it a week after we left, and a day before he and Elaine had themselves gone off for a tour in northern Europe and Scandinavia. It read:

> My dear James,
>   I have a feeling I owe you an apology and when you have read further you will understand why. The fact is, old boy, I got in touch with that Harley Street

chap I mentioned to you, and told him about your car accident and what I assumed to be certain after-effects. Well, to cut a long story short, he thought I was wrong, and if the police were not interested then certain other people might be, and he would see what he could do.

I will say no more, old boy, except to add that a certain Major Ricketts, who is a government official (so to speak), will be telephoning you, as he is *most interested*. He will be able to advise you, and, incidentally, make sure that the police give you proper protection in future.

Our love to Juliet and yourself, old boy,
STANLEY

CHAPTER 14

Ricketts, in the event, did not telephone till we had been back a week; until, in fact, the morning of the day when Stanley and Elaine Bristow were due back.

It was one of the longest weeks of my life. Just as, on holiday, the first days pass slowly, so that after three days it seems as though one had been away a week, so now, after our return, the days seemed to drag interminably.

On the one hand, I was watching the letter box and listening for a threatening voice on the telephone; on the other, I was waiting impatiently for Major Ricketts to get in touch with me.

Then, quite suddenly, he was on the 'phone, and arranging to meet me that same evening in the downstairs bar of the Ritz Hotel.

He was a tall, grey-haired man of about fifty, slim, with a good complexion, a straight nose, and a youthful smile. He wore a light tweed suit, a cream-coloured shirt, and a Gunners tie, and from time to time, as we talked, he made quick notes on the back of an envelope with an old-fashioned gold propelling pencil.

It is hard to describe the surge of relief I felt at being able to talk to somebody who took the matter seriously.

He began by saying that he had heard the rough outlines of my story, "indirectly from Mr. Bristow," as he put it, and asked me to repeat it very briefly. He listened attentively, and when I had given him a condensed version, he nodded his head enthusiastically.

"You know, of course, that some foreign governments go in for blackmail for espionage purposes?"

I stared at him and said:

"You're not suggesting that Mrs. Dawson, of the Bower Hotel, Burlington, was a spy, are you?"

"Rather the contrary."

"Meaning?"

"Meaning that I believe your theory about Mrs. Dawson."

"You do?"

I was watching him closely, waiting for the qualification. After a few seconds it came:

"Up to a point," he said.

"What point?" I asked, almost as soon as the words were out of his mouth.

"Up to the point where attempts were made to bribe, cajole, or threaten her into handing over the complete details of her black-mail victims—according to *my* theory, that is."

"Go on," I said.

"She had a warped mind, all right. Obsessed with the idea of hitting back at the criminal world. But when it came to hitting at her own country, the answer was, no. They made the wrong approach, I expect."

"Wrong approach?"

"'Help us destroy the class system which produced criminals and killed your husband'—that sort of thing. But it didn't work, did it?"

"No, it didn't work, assuming that was the line. That and money, I suppose?"

"They would have offered her compensation for loss of income, so to speak," said Ricketts grimly. "They're realistic, you know. Then came the final offer."

"In Pompeii," I muttered, and looked around at the luxurious decoration and thought of the dusty earth of Pompeii.

"In Pompeii," Ricketts said, and signalled for another drink for us. I said:

"Why kill her?"

"My department thinks," he began, and stopped.

"What is your department?" I asked.

"Does it matter?"

I shook my head, regretting my tactless question.

"My department thinks she was killed because somebody else came forward, offering the required information—for the same money."

"Who?" I asked, as if I hadn't guessed.

"Some intimate, personal assistant, who had access to her records, and who has probably now disappeared abroad."

I gazed into my whisky and soda. Then I said:

"Is Mrs. Gray still at the Bower Hotel?"

"Mrs. Gray is not still at that hotel. She has left the country."

"The muffin-faced old traitor," I said.

"We have no proof," said Ricketts primly.

"And me?"

"It's anybody's guess."

"Well, go on—guess," I pressed him.

"I guess your intervention came at a delicate, inconvenient juncture. A year, perhaps six months later, they might not have minded. I guess that all these threats had a purpose."

"I'm glad of that. That makes my day," I said bitterly, but he didn't smile. He said:

"These incidents were laid on so that if you discovered anything awkward neither the police nor anybody else would take you seriously. Your reputation would be that of a mentally unstable person. Understand?"

I nodded. But I said:

"Why not crooks? Why not commercial blackmail, a going concern, profitable, ready-made?"

"No mere criminal organisation would go to this trouble or expense. They'd have killed you."

"Why didn't this lot?"

"This lot, as you call them, they don't kill much, not if they can avoid it." He hesitated. Then he added: "But they will if they must. That's the view of my department."

"Meaning?" I asked, unnecessarily.

"Meaning they've been patient with you. Meaning it's as well we met."

I took a deep slug of whisky.

"It's as well we met," I said.

"You have been, and are, up against a hostile Intelligence Service, you realise that?"

I nodded, but said that I couldn't see either Miss Brett, or poor Bunface, or even chunky Bardoni gathering valuable secrets.

"Small fry," said Ricketts. "Afraid of your investigations for their own personal reasons. Afraid of their past catching up."

"Afraid of a desolate future," I murmured, and he nodded.

"But here and there among Mrs. Dawson's victims there must be others, equally afraid, but more importantly situated. She'd been at it a long time, Mr. Compton."

"Why me?" I asked after a pause. "Why did they think I'd find out things the Italian and British police wouldn't find out?"

Ricketts smiled.

"Divided police forces, divided responsibilities, divided access to information, I think that's the answer, don't you? The Italian police were in charge of investigations. They had no reason to know the cause and motive lay buried in her past, in England. Doubtless they sent a routine request for background information to Scotland Yard—and that's probably just what they got, general background information and no more. The British police probably thought the motive and clues were to be found in Italy. Why shouldn't they think so? Anyway, it wasn't their case. Then you, bumbling along obstinately, began to creep up on things, and that wouldn't do, would it?"

I watched him call for the bill.

"What do you want me to do?" I asked.

"Nothing," said Ricketts gravely. "I think it's a bit out of your league table. You don't want the whole thing to start up again."

Once again, and for the last time in this affair, I felt the old, old bloody-mindedness boiling up inside me.

"Oh, I'm not going to drop it now, not now that I've got some idea of what it's all about. I'll go on sniffing around a bit," I muttered.

"I can't stop you," said Ricketts, and smiled again. "But if there's any trouble let me know."

"Too damn true, I will," I said.

When we parted I had agreed to write down on paper every smallest detail of what I could remember of the affair, and deliver the document to his personal address the following morning. He thought it safer not to call at my house.

I took a taxi home, rejoicing that I had not succumbed to the temptation to put the red geranium in the front window.

Juliet was delighted, too, and we worked on the document until two o'clock in the morning.

At ten o'clock I drove round to Hurley Mews, of Belgrave Square, and found his number, 25, and saw it painted on the door.

At first I thought I had gone to the wrong house. The window panes were broken or missing. The interior looked gutted, the paper hanging in shreds on the walls.

When I had checked the number with the address he had written for me I thought I might as well ring the bell, but it didn't work, of course, so I knocked. It was quiet in the mews, and very deserted, considering the time of day.

When there was no reply, I tried the door, and found it unlocked. I went in, not knowing quite what to do.

In the event, I didn't have to do anything much, except gaze for a moment at the dusty, uncarpeted stairs, because inside, on the floor, was a buff-coloured envelope addressed to me.

It was typed on my own machine, of course, like the other notes, prepared in advance for just such a contingency. The message was quite short:

> I told you the truth. We have been very patient
> with you. It is as well we met.
>
>   Ricketts.

I stared at it, feeling suddenly sick. And then dizzy; and then neither sick nor dizzy but just numb, my brain refusing to function clearly.

Then my heart started beating very fast indeed. I did not tremble, but I heard my heart beats growing louder and louder in my ears.

After a while I tried to think.

I saw now the three lines of defence.

First, the self-generated attempts by the little fish to save themselves; then the partial truth, revealed by Col. Pearson; finally the full truth, told me to my face, blatantly, by the man calling himself Ricketts.

I stared down at the note again, re-reading it, while the fear pain, which is not exactly a pain, but more of a muscular contraction, caught me in the stomach.

Outside, a late autumn breeze blew gustily, the hanging, shredded wallpaper rustled. A little trickle of plaster detached by the wind dropped at my feet, as if it had fallen from the nest of some animal.

The peasant, even the humblest peasant, particularly the humblest peasant, thinks he is safe in his obscurity and comparative anonymity. Let me be, he says, let me till the soil and I will mind no other business but my own, but he never was, never is and never will be safe, I thought.

One innocent, unlucky step, even on the well-trodden paths, and he comes within the scrutiny of the eyes in the surrounding jungle, and if he is alert he can hear the faint crackle of twigs and the slither of the hidden bodies in the undergrowth. He does well to shift his spear forward, and make the sign of the Cross, or glance towards Mecca, or finger his sacred, pagan amulet.

Men must fight, and some will win and some will lose, as I had lost.

For the greater the cause, in the end, the greater the tyranny which it erects to defend itself. Before the noble and good concept of complete democracy a man might travel where he wished in the world, without much let or hindrance, whereas now he was boxed in by frontiers, passports, and visas and walls, and interdicts, and laws, and police, to preserve the liberty and freedom of the individual.

And under some monarchies it was permissible to cry, "Down with the monarchy!" and under some democracies it was forbidden to cry "Down with democracy!" and under dictatorships it was forbidden to cry "Down with dictatorships!" and it was all, all in the interests of the freedom of the individual.

So the peasant must be vigilant, taking care not to be pushed around, and if necessary the peasant must fight, as he always has done, even though his fight end in martyrdom, or is brief and unheroic, as mine had been. It all helps.

Did I really think all this, as I read the note from the man calling himself Ricketts?

Certainly not.

It was thought out and disentangled afterwards. But at such moments there is an exploding germ, a chaotic, expanding universe of logic and emotion, which contains within itself the essentials for future dissection, and this I experienced.

This, too, I did think, in sadness and despair: the tribe is so busy protecting the tribe, that it has no time to protect the individual.

Then I felt upon my neck an increasing coolness, as the street door was opened more widely. But before I could turn round I was struck on the nape of the neck, not by an instrument, but by a hand which hurled me so violently forward that I staggered and fell at the foot of the stairs.

I looked up from the dust, still clutching the note in one hand, and in the other doorway I saw Ricketts, still wearing his Gunners tie, and the man who called himself Sergeant Matthews, with his good-natured, brown bovine eyes, and two other men, one in a knee-length leather jacket, whom I recognised.

Ricketts said:

"You haven't been playing fair with us, have you?"

I made no reply.

It is tempting to put into my mouth, in retrospect, some telling riposte. But I said nothing, because I was too afraid. I would like to explain that feeling. It was partly a natural fear of death, but partly also because I had a vision of Juliet waiting for me, and the hours passing, and Juliet still waiting.

"We have been very patient—haven't we?" said Ricketts, and kicked me in the ribs. "Well, haven't we?" he asked again, and kicked me again.

I nodded. He said:

"I can slug you and gag you and tie you, and put you in a crate which is upstairs, or you can come voluntarily with us in the back of the van outside. Which do you want?"

"I'll come," I said.

"Well, get up then. Go on, get up."

I got to my feet slowly. Grimy. Dazed. Beyond hope. Thinking of the red geranium.

I heard him say:

"This man's got a pistol with a silencer."

I nodded.

I stumbled towards the door, and the group parted, and then closed round me. Outside stood a nondescript green van. I had not heard it draw up. I climbed into the back. There was no partition between the back and the driver's seat. I waited for the others to get in.

The van had no side windows, and there were no seats at the back. Brown-eyed Matthews and a fourth character, a squat, sallow-skinned type, waited to climb in after me. Sallow-Face motioned me to sit on the floor. Brown-Eyes slumped down opposite me. He caught my eye for a second, gave an almost apologetic half-smile, shrugged, and looked away. I saw Leather-Jacket open the driver's door, and Ricketts by the opposite door. Ricketts was saying something to Sallow-Face, who had paused by the rear door of the van.

Through the windscreen I saw a big, dark-blue van manoeu-vring to turn in the narrow mews about twenty yards away. It seemed to be having some difficulty. In fact, when it was broadside on it stayed that way, as though the engine had stalled, though in fact the engine had probably been switched off, because almost at once four men in plain clothes jumped out of the back and began to approach us at a sort of half-run, half-walk speed.

Leather-Jacket glanced at them, then flicked his head round and looked in the other direction, and then shouted something, and looking through the rear of the van I saw the exit from the opposite end of the mews blocked by two black cars, shining, meticulously clean, side by side, fronts pointed towards us. Four other plain-clothes men were approaching from that direction, at the same half-run, half-walk speed. I could see them quite clearly because Sallow-Face was no longer blocking the view at the rear of the van.

Ricketts and Leather-Jacket had slid momentarily out of sight, but I heard the thud of their feet as they pounded back to the house. It took Brown-Eyes a few seconds to gather what was happening. He was fumbling with a cigarette packet at the time. Maybe he didn't understand the language, anyway.

This was a pity for him, one way and another.

By the time he got around to bundling himself out of the van and legging it towards the house, the first shots were being fired, and I saw one of the Special Branch officers stagger and fall.

English cops don't normally carry arms. Perhaps in a country where, unlike America, the citizenry do not have a traditional right to bear arms, the cops think they should set an example. But now and again, if real trouble is possible, pistols will grudgingly and sparingly be issued. The present lot had one gun for each team of four, and as they didn't much like seeing a colleague picked off, they began to shoot back.

I was lying on the floor of the van by this time to avoid ricochets. Pretty dazed and confused. But I could see the door of the house closing just as Brown-Eyes was scuttling up the steps. He collapsed in a heap on the doorstep. Maybe they didn't know he was so near, maybe they did, and didn't care because he was British and they weren't, I thought. Expendable Brown-Eyes.

Now there was a lull for a minute or two, as though everybody was thinking things out. The Special Branch police had grabbed their wounded colleague, and were standing flat against the doors of neighbouring houses. People in the little mews houses were opening windows and peering out. A loud-hailer on one of the police cars started up:

"Keep away from your windows, please! Please stay indoors! Keep away from your windows and stay indoors, please!"

There was another short pause and then it started up again: "To House No. 25, Hurley Mews—come out with your hands raised. The house is surrounded. You cannot escape. Come out with your hands raised at once."

When there was no response after a full minute, they repeated the words, this time adding: "If you do not come out, we shall fire smoke and tear-gas and come and get you. You may be shot. Escape is impossible."

But there was no response. At both ends of the mews I saw a small crowd being kept back by uniformed police.

The police waited five minutes without saying or doing anything. This is sound psychologically. It gives time for feelings of defiance to cool off.

At the end of that time they repeated the instructions, very slowly, adding, "You have sixty seconds to obey this order."

But while the loud-hailer was still booming, and without the use of tear-gas or smoke, two officers were edging along close to the wall, guns in hands, until they reached the door. Here they paused and were joined by two more, one carrying an axe.

I watched the big axe rise and fall once on the wood around the lock and heard the crash as the shoulders of two fourteen-stone

Special Branch officers completed the job, and I saw them disappear inside and waited for the sound of shots and shouts. None came. Nothing seemed to happen in the house.

But something happened outside the house all right. Two police officers rushed the van a few moments after the others had rushed the house. One of them, as I rose to my feet, bending low because of the van roof, flung himself at my legs in a football tackle, bringing me crashing to the floor. He was taking no chances.

"God Almighty, are you daft? Have you gone off your rocker?" I shouted.

"Probably," he said. "Come on, hop out, there's a good chap."

"What the hell have I done?"

"You're being detained on suspicion of passing information of possible use to a potential enemy, contrary to the Official Secrets Acts—something like that; come on, get cracking."

I saw him pick up the envelope containing the document I had prepared for Ricketts. Somebody must have brought it into the green van. Maybe Brown-Eyes Matthews. If so, it was the last thing he carried. Later I saw his body being borne to an ambulance. He hadn't been shot by police bullets as he tried to get into the house. He had been shot in the chest from inside the closing door. A man who might talk too much, on his own, inside Britain, and be an encumbrance outside Britain. Expendable, and better dead. Meanwhile, Ricketts and Leather-Jacket and Sallow-Face had vanished.

I thought something was wrong when a man I later knew as Chief Inspector Hope came out of the house alone. He looked grim.

I saw him run to the two police cars, and immediately their engines started and they roared off, sirens sounding, braying like castrated donkeys. The uniformed police at one end of the mews pushed the crowd back to let them race through and round the corner to the main road, tyres screeching.

House No. 25 had no rear exit. It backed on to another house. It could not be surrounded in the real sense of the word. No. 26 was the same. But No. 27 had a back door leading to an alley. Ricketts had a five-year lease on all three, through an innocent nominee who had sub-let the houses to him. Two roughly made communicating doors, for just such an emergency, connected the three houses. The birds had flown through the alley. All except the dead pigeon.

There are many little private landing places in Britain from which a small aeroplane can take off, and others on the Continent where it can land. Chief Inspector Hope did not bother to alert Interpol. He didn't need to. He knew exactly where Ricketts was heading, and the time and place of his rendezvous in forty-eight hours' time.

He telephoned the Naples police, and booked two seats on a Comet, one for himself and one for an Italian-speaking sergeant on his staff.

I offered to go if the police would pay my fare, on the feeble excuse that I might help in identifying people, but it wouldn't wash. He said he'd had them under observation long enough for his purposes. The police are a bit mean about spending public money.

But I heard what happened, of course, and I can just imagine old muffin-faced Mrs. Caroline Gray stumping up from the little railway station, fighting off guides, through the gloomy Porta Marina of Pompeii, along the Via Marina, then turning left, past the Forum, along by the Insula Occidentalis and out by the Porta Ercolano to the Way of the Tombs. Shortly, turning left, then right, she would have been almost there, at the House of the Mysteries.

A long walk for an elderly woman, short, bandy-legged, and solidly built, fattened on Bower Hotel food. Ricketts could have directed her by a shorter route, but as her mission was to retrieve a certain address book from Bardoni's hotel, I think he chose the longer route because it led her past House No. 27, in Section 12, where Mrs. Dawson had died. A kind of reminder to her not to have second thoughts.

The Way of the Tombs also made her pensive. She saw the great monumental mausoleum of the family Istacides, with a round colonnade on top, the marble tomb of Munatius Faustus with its bas-relief of a tempest-tossed ship and struggling crew, the semi-circular exedra of Mamia Publius, a priestess of the people, on land voted for the purpose by the Senate, and the imposing last resting places of Marcus Porcius, and of Aulus Umbricius Scaurus, magistrate and merchant, to whom the Senate had not only voted land for the monument, but 200 sesterces for funeral money, and an equestrian statue in the Forum. All these honours are engraved on the sepulchre. An important man, Scaurus. She saw these and many other tombs.

The early Romans took the ashes of their dead to places outside the city and built their monuments, often with seats for visitors or passers-by, near to roads which would be thronged with travellers. Here the lingering spirits of the dead could happily listen to the chit-chat of the living. A nice thought, but Mrs. Caroline Gray was not in the mood for chit-chat, either with the living or the dead.

The main reason for this was the fact that she had not brought the address book with her.

I like to think of her standing in the initiation chamber where the Dionysiac mysteries were enacted, gazing around at the fresco with its life-size female figures which give some clue to the nature of the initiation ceremony.

Dumpy, beady-eyed, incongruous in such surroundings, she was alone, for it was late in the day. I can confirm, as can most others who have been there, that this room exudes an atmosphere of age-old occultism which is by no means due to the fresco with its portrayal of the ceremony, its Mistress in charge, its masks of Bacchus and Ariadne, its flagellation, and frenzied dance by the nude girl initiate.

She had about five minutes to decide whether she would like to have been an initiate herself. Then she heard footsteps and turned and saw Leather-Jacket and Sallow-Face.

Whether Ricketts was suspicious, whether he had noted that there were rather more so-called guards than usual around the House of the Mysteries, it is not now possible to say. He remained by the exit; till his bodyguard, perhaps, had tested the ground.

When the Italian police closed in on Mrs. Gray and the other two, he turned and ran for it, doubtless because in Italy he did not have the same diplomatic privilege as in England.

The Italian police did not use their guns until, in the Way of the Tombs, he began to use his.

He fell and died by the tomb of Aulus Veius, a magistrate, appropriately enough.

It is always hard for a writer to rehabilitate a villain, or a person he has regarded as a villain, even a minor one. One has lived with the villain, one has set ideas about the villain, one is loath to discard them.

But facts are facts, and facts from Chief Inspector Hope cannot be ignored.

I am bound therefore to record that Mrs. Caroline Gray, now living quietly once more at the Bower Hotel, was not a money-grabbing traitor. I must state, though reluctantly, that she knew nothing of Mrs. Dawson's activities, and that the tip-off came first from a terrified Bardoni to the Italian police, who passed it on to England.

Thereafter, Mrs. Caroline Gray acted under directions from the Special Branch of Scotland Yard. They have little to do with Criminal Investigations Departments, such as the police who interviewed me.

They detect espionage and such important things. They don't deal in petty crime like murders, bank robberies, and train robberies.

They are cats that walk alone.

For me, the slice of terror, which is all that it was, lay in the thickness of the slice: the peasant is surrounded by more than he imagines. Behind the eyes which observe him are yet others, which observe those eyes in their turn, and behind the predators slithering in the undergrowth are yet others, stalking the predators. The slice is thick and fearful.

We live in dangerous times. All one can do is keep the spear ready, and a feeble thing it is, touch the amulet, and hope for the best, and trust that, as in my case, the tribe can after all protect not only the tribe but the individual.

There is no harm in hoping.

To be on the safe side, I always, even now, keep a red geranium on the window sill.

Note

Since I have to make the best I can of my dolt of a so-called father-in-law, and ghastly mother-in-law, I have changed all the names and one or two other circumstances in this story. It is not even published under my own name.

Also by John Bingham
With a new introduction by his protégé, John le Carré

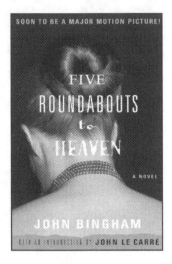

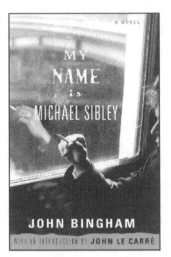

When Peter Harding and Philip Bartels meet up again in the French countryside of their youth, the history—and the dark secrets it holds—is still there. The two share more than a friendship: stuck in a disenchanted marriage to his distant wife, Philip meets and falls in love with the graceful Lorna Dickson. Philip decides to poison his wife; however, unbeknownst to him, Peter and Lorna have fallen in love with each other. A chilling psychological study of how murder can so easily enter the minds of ordinary people.

Told through the eyes of a man accused of murder, *My Name Is Michael Sibley* was the first novel written by John Bingham. The news that John Prosset had been found dead in his isolated country cottage had come as quite a shock to his old friend Michael Sibley, for he had been staying with Prosset only that weekend. But a bigger shock awaits him when two police officers arrive at his door. For Prosset, it seems, was bludgeoned to death. And that is when Michael Sibley makes the first of many fateful mistakes— and begins on a path of deceit that will draw him closer to the hangman's noose. . . .

Available wherever books are sold or at www.simonsays.com

Printed in the United States
By Bookmasters